DEEP
IN THE
FOREST

DOUGLAS YOUNG

NEWMAN SPRINGS PUBLISHING
320 Broad Street
Red Bank, NJ 07701

First originally published by Newman Springs Publishing 2020

ISBN 978-1-63692-116-7 (Paperback)
ISBN 978-1-63692-117-4 (Digital)

Printed in the United States of America

For Parker, Joy, and Cory Young for a lifetime of love and support, and for the one who stayed but wants to remain backstage.

ACKNOWLEDGMENTS

For their influence, the author thanks Dr. Parker Young, Joy Young, Cory Young, Dr. Karen Dodson, Dr. Don Gehring, the Rev. Dr. Charles Hasty, Gina Lynne, Natalie Marks, Casandra McClellan, Amy Milligan, Geraldine Parrish, Libby Parrish, Richard Pilcher, Kenley Pope, the Rev. Dr. Jack Presseau, Dr. Scheryl Rutland, Essielya Scarbrough, Dr. Bob Thornton, Terry Wright, Dr. Chungeng Zhu, and the one who still prefers backstage.

CHAPTER 1

Driving home from work late on a Friday afternoon was usually one of the happiest times of the week for thirty-five-year-old Elton Peabody. The nervous tapping of his left foot aside, he was proud of working harder and longer than any other teacher at the high school, and he enjoyed reviewing both the week's successes and lessons learned as he made the fifteen-minute trip home. How he relished his small town's many tall oak trees and red, pink, and purple azaleas already in bloom. This third week in March had been unusually good since he judged his lectures to have been especially strong and the discussions lively and well-reasoned. His Western Civilization students seemed particularly taken with the dramas of the French Revolution, and he was delighted they appeared to appreciate the dangers posed by any kind of zealous purists. He had also finished grading his US History class term papers and was pleased with how relatively well most read. Nor had there been a single unpleasant encounter with students, colleagues, or any of the dreaded educrats (administrators). It had been just the kind of week to put him in an ideal frame of mind to hopefully make a fun weekend.

He and sweet old Mrs. Turner waved at each other as he turned into his neighborhood, a middle class mix of homes with no consistency of architecture. The auto-pilot ritual was repeated several times with other residents working in their yards as he made his way home.

"Easy, boy!" he laughed as General Longstreet tried to climb his leg upon entering the front door. Elton never failed to smile as the big fellow never failed to greet him with the same excited joy. But he soon realized Longstreet's enthusiasm was likely heightened by an overdue need to relieve himself since it was now 6:40. So Elton let him into the backyard and started to heat up supper in the microwave oven.

He had not been in the kitchen five minutes before hearing Longstreet bark with an urgency he had not heard before. What was unusual was the barks were punctuated by a strange, low growl Elton had only heard once before when Longstreet spotted a water moccasin on a fishing trip. Even stranger, the barks and growls were occasionally interrupted by a crying whimper Elton had rarely heard and never amidst barks and growls.

So he stuck his head out the sliding glass door to see what the matter was. But now he heard other dogs barking too and in what sounded like a borderline hysterical tone. Suddenly his houselights went out and the Count Basie record he had put on stopped. "Dadgummit," he uttered. Without the music, he noticed Longstreet's barking had grown more intense. Going outside to confirm the neighbors had lost power too, he realized their dogs' barking had ratcheted up as well, only now it sounded as if every canine in the county was in an uproar. With twilight taking hold, and hoping Longstreet would shut up in the house if distracted by a meal with the curtains drawn, Elton called him inside.

Except his dog ignored him. Thinking perhaps the general did not hear his calls for all the barking, he went out in the yard to lead him back inside. But Longstreet was singularly intent on warning away whatever had alarmed him. Only when Elton pulled him by his collar did he finally, grudgingly, return to the house, albeit with many parting barks, grunts, growls, and cries along the way. Back inside, Elton tried to calm his dog who was now crouched on the carpet staring intently at the closed curtains while whining softly.

"What's wrong, boy? You're a general. You've got nothing to fear. Settle down, big fellow."

But even with his favorite bowl of food placed before him, Longstreet remained fixed on something beyond the curtains, not even looking at the meal. Never having seen such behavior, Elton stared at him before turning toward the curtains himself.

Now dark outside, he noticed a faint glow not seen before. This was odd since behind his home stood woods for a great many acres crowded with pines, oaks, and dogwoods. He drew back the curtain to confirm a distinct light emanating from somewhere deep in the forest. Unable to discern its shape or form, he strained at what the source could be amidst so many tall trees and thick brush. The one time he walked through the wilderness had revealed no roads or trails within it. There were a few small clearings, but no access to them except by walking.

Could a neighbor be traversing the woods with a flashlight to see what upset the dogs? But he had never seen anyone go into that thicket. Indeed, he liked how most of his neighbors were quiet retirees. They regularly walked the neighborhood sidewalks but would not venture beyond their backyard fences. Besides, the light was like a large, bright cloud ensconced somewhere way back in the forest, emanating far too much light for a flashlight.

Standing by the large glass door, he noticed how Longstreet was whining louder and emitting sounds Elton had not heard before. Looking back toward the trees, it seemed the light was becoming more intense. Perhaps that was just due to it now being nightfall, but he was not sure.

With no television or musical distractions, not caring to read by flashlight, and satisfied his dog had relieved himself outside and was now safely inside with plenty of food, Elton focused on the strange illumination. He had forgotten how hungry he was and decided to investigate this mystery in the woods.

So he grabbed a flashlight and started for the door. But as soon as he slid it open, Longstreet barked and leapt on his leg. Never had Elton seen him display such a desperate yearning for his master to stay. Yet when given the chance to join him outside, his canine friend refused. When Elton turned to step on the back patio, Longstreet's teeth grabbed the bottom of his pants leg to try to pull him back inside.

"Whoa, boy! What's wrong with you? Back off! It's all right."

Longstreet had never acted anything like this. When Elton finally jerked his pants leg loose to quickly close the door behind him, he was more stunned than angered to see part of the fabric was gone. He chose to be grateful his dog had not bitten him but instead sought to protect him. Yet the thought of taking Longstreet in his present state on a leash into the forest did not seem wise. At this point his canine buddy would not go anyway.

So Elton went toward the woods on his own, able to hear Longstreet wailing in the house. He climbed over the back fence, turned on the flashlight, and followed in the direction of the distant luster. He briefly looked back toward the neighborhood to see if anyone else was venturing outside to seek out the light but found no company. Instead, he saw what appeared to be the glow of candles in homes. And there was still a cacophony of barks echoing throughout the subdivision.

Peering ahead into the forest, he realized its trees were too thick to navigate very fast, and his flashlight failed to find any undiscovered trail. The glow in the distance was becoming brighter but remained stubbornly far away. As the neighborhood barking grew more muffled, he began to feel a strange quiet creeping over him. In fact, when he could no longer hear the dogs, he listened for the sounds of the forest. But there was none. He heard not one cricket chirping or a single owl hooting. Nor did he hear any bullfrog. So he just listened and felt his stomach muscles slowly tighten with the realization he was completely enveloped by silence.

Turning back toward the glare, he saw it had grown not only brighter but was giving off pulsating waves of light. He became transfixed by this throbbing, gleaming glow.

Moving toward it, he tried to guess what it was. Could some folks have decided to camp in one of the least developed areas of the county? Might this just be a large group of campers in a clearing with several campfires or a generator producing extremely bright light?

Dear Lord, please don't let it be a bunch of students from the school, particularly from any of my classes, he thought. How embarrassing if they saw Mr. Peabody emerge from the trees. And what a nightmare if they were drinking or smoking dope. He could well imagine wild rumors flying around the school come Monday about that young history teacher hanging out with his partying students. That had career-altering implications.

However, something told him there were no students ahead since he heard no loud music or teenage laughs or squeals. Still, what was it?

He realized the light was not only becoming more intense but larger. What had been a distant glow was now much wider and taller in scope. And he thought he heard a dull hum now. In fact, as the glittering white light got closer, he realized the sounds of leaves and pine straw below his feet could barely be heard for the growing buzz that appeared to be produced by whatever was making the light.

Staring ahead, he could see an open space where the light was most intense. Brilliantly bright beams of throbbing light now cut between the trees. So vivid was the light that even the backsides of the trees were illuminated.

Elton also saw that, despite all the trees still between himself and the light, his clothes were now lit up. In fact, they were glowing like the time he took his school's Presbyterian Club students to the bowling alley for "cosmic bowling." The place had been lit only by strobe lights which caused lightly colored patches of clothing to glimmer in the dark. Yet his clothes were gleaming much more intensely now, and he was not even wearing white.

He also began to feel warmer. Checking his watch, he saw it had stopped at 6:54, even though he felt sure it had to be well after seven. How could an electric power outage have done that?

It was then he felt a big flock of butterflies flutter in his gut, as they did at times of deep dread. For the first time that evening, he felt fear.

With the light just beyond the trees ahead, Elton had no reference for what emerged before him. The clearing contained about one hundred square yards and was entirely aglow with the brightest white light he had ever seen. His entire field of vision was consumed by the feverish light, now accompanied by a roaring chorus of hums at a deafening decibel.

Mighty tempted to run away, he was still determined to see what this was before setting a speed record for exiting a forest. Slowly making his way to the last tree before the opening, he gripped it tightly with his head buried behind it. He saw how incredibly lit up the whole area was and well into the forest.

Not understanding why, he gradually moved into the light. There had to be a reasonable explanation for this, he kept telling himself. Otherwise, nothing made sense. Moving a few steps into the cauldron of light, he had to squint. Looking down, even the ground was ablaze in white, and the roar was completely upon him. He felt as if he were drowning in a pool of pure light and sound. He wanted to run back into the woods but felt frozen and disoriented. His heart pounded like a deck of cards being shuffled. Was he risking a heart attack?

It was then he noticed the light turning colors in places: flashes of deep red, blue, yellow, orange, purple, and green streaked around him. He felt as if he were trapped in a kaleidoscope of sheer light surrounded by a wall of noise. Time appeared stuck, and he feared he had been sucked into some kind of space-time wormhole. He blinked and dared to look into the light but only saw endless waves of acutely white light freckled with vivid colors.

He could neither move forward nor backward. He could not move at all. It was as if he were stuck in a continuum of light without end in all directions. Never had he felt so totally trapped and absolutely alone. Shaking and struggling to breathe, he realized he had reached a state of panic.

Was this some type of religious experience? Could there be angels or the wheels of Ezekiel here? Yet he felt nothing but terror and could not believe the God he worshipped at First Presbyterian Church had anything to do with this.

So was this something evil? Though the gems of colored light looked celestial, he detected no heavenly vibes and hardly saw this as a friendly welcome. Yet he had sought out the light, not the reverse, and nothing or no one had touched him in anger.

Had he died? Was he transitioning to another world? If so, why was it taking so long? "Please, dear God, just send me to heaven or hell," he pleaded. "Anything but this." Or had he already entered hell?

Was this an alien spacecraft, a bona fide unidentified flying object from another planet? Maybe, but where was the ship? And where were the proverbial "little green men?"

And where was anyone? How could it be of the twenty thousand residents of Johnston County, only one Elton Peabody had seen or heard this thing and sought it out? Where was everybody?

Unable to move and captured by a fear more ferocious than any he had ever felt, he could barely think. Words would not come, aloud or even in his mind. *Think of something,* he kept telling himself. He started yelling but heard nothing above the din of noise and could no longer tell if he was making sounds.

It was then he collapsed to his knees and clasped his hands to his bowed head. He fervently, desperately wanted to pray but could not even recall the Lord's Prayer. He tried to just think of God and something to say. Frightened beyond words, he finally whispered, "Please, dear God. Please help me. I'm so sorry for all my sins. Please save me."

Perceiving he could not get any more afraid, he resigned himself to his fate. Without consciously deciding to do so, he found himself on the ground in a fetal ball, hugging his knees and shaking with his eyes shut tight. Yet the light still pierced his eyelids.

At one point he closed his eyes as firmly as he could and then opened them wide to wake up from a nightmare, as he had done so often before. But opening his eyes only caused them to immediately close again, as if stabbed by the merciless light. And no matter how hard he pressed his hands over his ears, his head sounded like an echo chamber of jet engines.

Having lost the capacity to reason, his mind clung fiercely to a blessed refuge of nothingness, a commitment to ride this ear-shattering light storm out and just accept whatever happened. He did not know if he went to sleep, passed out, or hallucinated. He had no sense of how long he was feverishly holding himself. He just shook and rocked back and forth in a steady rhythm to push against the fear and try to prevent thought.

CHAPTER

When he awoke, the absolute silence startled him. He seemed unable to process it. Though his eyes remained closed, he no longer sensed any light. Slowly he opened them to see only dark. For an instant he hoped he was waking from the worst nightmare of his life. But the pine straw stuck to his shirt shattered that notion. Turning on his back, he saw only stars in a night sky as wondrously calm as his previous experience had been hellish. He dared to lift his head and look at the clearing and surrounding trees. All appeared completely, eerily normal. But he still shook and could now hear his teeth chatter. He wanted to get up and run home, but the thought of going anywhere or facing anything was too much. Not now. Not yet. The forest was utterly dark and appeared foreboding. Who knew where the light went? Perhaps it had found another lair and just wanted to lure him to it again.

It was then he heard the crickets for the first time that night. He had never thought much about them before, but now relished their songs as the most comforting sounds on the planet. Suddenly he heard a whole chorus of owls hooting more excitedly than he could ever recall. Gently he sat up to try to reorient himself.

A slow scan of the clearing showed there was not a single light anywhere and nary a sound aside from crickets and the cacophony of competing hoot owls. Though still shaking, he wondered if his ordeal was over. Did he dare believe it was all done? The beginnings of the most magnificent sense of relief began to wash over him. He was alive and, examining his body, without injury too.

But just as he felt his heartbeat start to slow, his now hair-trigger sense of danger heard what appeared to be voices through the trees, and coming his way. Soon he saw what he now recoiled from more than anything—lights. Narrow little beams moving from right to left were approaching him. Though his head said they were flashlights, his heart began to race again, as did the shakes. Thus, he sat staring wide-eyed at the lights entering the clearing. As several crossed his face, his body jumped and he heard himself loudly gasp.

Then he definitely heard voices. Voices he knew. Well.

"Hey, somebody's there, y'all. Hello! We're with the Johnston County Sheriff's Department. I'm Sheriff Beauregard Peabody. We got a bunch of calls about a bright light in the woods."

Elton's brother was a big man who had been an all-state line-backer on the local high school football team. He went on to earn a criminal justice degree in college and became a deputy on the force at twenty-two. Four years ago, at twenty-nine, he was elected the county's youngest-ever top lawman when old Sheriff Speaky Stevens retired after thirty-two years in charge. With Sheriff Peabody were five deputies and several self-described "concerned citizens" who wanted a piece of the evening's excitement. They rushed over to the terrified disheveled man clutching himself and looking at them with eyes that pleaded for mercy.

"Ah! Ah!" he cried as the party reached him.

"Bo, it's Elton!" Deputy Sheriff A.P. Hill exclaimed.

"Elton, what's wrong? What are you doing here? What's going on?" the sheriff asked.

But his elder brother's eyes still beheld all of them with fear and started to water. When Bo bent down to lift him up, Elton jumped.

"It's okay, brother. Everything's fine. It's me, Bo. We're all friends here. Look, there's A.P. Here's Rufus. You know Tommy Skidmore. Remember Jimmy Taylor?"

Several men eagerly sought to assure Elton that all was fine. Everyone knew the sheriff's older brother as the nerdish sibling who was a popular history teacher at Johnston High. He had taught a few of them. He was also one of the last folks anyone expected to see in the middle of the woods at night where they had earlier seen that incredibly bright light.

As Bo and A.P. raised him to his feet, Elton looked straight ahead with cartoonishly wide eyes. His whole body was mildly convulsing, and he answered none of the questions eagerly asked of him.

"All right, let's just sit him down and let him set a spell," Bo commanded.

As Elton clutched his knees, shaking and slowly rocking, his younger brother sat by him with a hand on his shoulder, softly repeating that everything was okay. But as soon as the shaking was almost gone, Deputy Hill turned on his flashlight to examine him. The instant his face lit up, Elton gasped and jumped back.

"Not now, A.P.," Bo said, and the flashlight went out. Now both of the sheriff's large hands slowly massaged Elton's shoulders as he and his top deputy repeated the mantra he was with friends and everyone was safe.

The other men inspecting the clearing compared their finds. Though the amazingly bright light they saw emanating from this spot a short time ago had vanished, they noted how the ground had clearly been disturbed. The grass, pine cones, bushes, and two seedlings were all flattened. The damage appeared fresh. Some of the grass and pine straw also looked burnt, and here and there were small piles of what resembled pale yellow sand.

"Somebody did this," Deputy Rufus Pike declared. "Somebody or something flattened this whole area, and real recent too."

As the posse looked closely at the broken limbs to try to determine the culprit, Elton turned toward his brother and studied him at length. Bo mustered a concerned smile and patted his back. After a couple of minutes, Elton at last started to speak.

"Bo, I've never been so scared in my whole life. I can't convey how terrifying it all was. It was the brightest, loudest thing imaginable. I still don't know what it was."

"It's okay, man. It's gone now. We saw it too…and heard it."

"A loud buzz?"

"Loudest I've ever heard."

Hearing them talk, some of the others came over to ask Elton how he was.

"He's all right, boys. Let him be," the sheriff announced. "Elton, we got a ton of calls from folks all over about lights in the sky and a slew of them about some super bright light in the woods, especially from your neighborhood: Thelma Turner, old Miss Whitley…even Rev. Presseau. So we all drove over and, sure enough, we could see something glowing through the trees. So we got on foot and just started following the light. It kept getting brighter and then we all heard this loud hum. But before we could get to it, it just vanished. The light and sound both."

As he snapped his fingers, Elton jumped slightly but was now self-conscious enough to try to hide his fear. He had been listening intently to his brother with a mix of relief he had not gone insane coupled with the fear this was real, which meant it could happen again.

"Boys, let's get some pictures, put some of this yellow stuff in a bag, and take a couple of these flattened bushes back to the station. I don't think there's anything more to see here. Show's over," the sheriff pronounced. "A.P., stay close to this part of town the rest of the evening. Elton, let's go."

While the others talked animatedly on the trek back to their cars, Elton remained quiet but listened intently. Bo walked alongside him but was too preoccupied with his brother's fragile state to hear the excited speculation. He weighed the strange sights and sounds of this call with his brother's emotionally frayed history. A lot of people could attest to a lot of weird things tonight, but could his brother be having another nervous breakdown? That offered the prospect of a return of all kinds of unwanted family stress. *Focus on my job, keep everyone calm, and go one step at a time,* he repeated to himself.

On the drive back to the sheriff's department, everyone in the squad cars noticed a lot more traffic than usual, as well as congregations of folks in yards looking at the clouds. On three occasions, Sheriff Peabody saw folks leaning against their car or pick-up with shotguns aimed skyward. Each time he pulled over and told them they could look at the sky all night long, but needed to put away their guns. It was his considered judgment there would be no alien invasion tonight and, even if there was, shotguns might not offer a sufficient defense.

Though Bo generally wanted his young deputies to get experience interviewing witnesses, he took charge tonight. To put Elton at ease, he and Deputy Otis Cummings questioned him in the sheriff's office instead of the interrogation room. Cummings had been a star quarterback on the Johnston High School football team and the first black deputy Sheriff Peabody hired in his first months in office. He was perhaps the most popular deputy in the black and white communities.

"Can we get you anything, Elton?" Deputy Cummings asked. "Coke, coffee, donuts?"

"No thanks, Otis."

"Elton, just please tell us everything that happened tonight from the start, and take your time," instructed his brother.

The whole story was recounted in detail. Elton was no longer shaking but still felt dazed. It was as if he was mired in jet lag or slightly woozy from prescription drugs. His speech was softer and less animated than normal, and he had a hard time making eye contact as his story got stranger. No one interrupted him while the tape recorder quietly documented his account. When he finished, Bo hit the Stop button, and everyone was silent.

"I'm real sorry this happened, Elton. It's bizarre for everybody. And you sure ain't the only one to see and hear some mighty strange goings-on tonight."

"What do you think it was?" his brother asked. As was his wont, the sheriff would not bite until confident he had enough evidence to back up his assessment. Experience had taught him any speculation on his part could easily distort the direction of an investigation and, on occasion, leak into the community.

"I just can't say. I don't rightly know, Elton. I know you saw something. We all did. And it was the most freakish, frightening thing you ever came across. But there's just not enough evidence for any kind of theory as to what it was."

"A lot of folks think that thing was a UFO," Otis volunteered. "There've been reports of UFOs tonight in Johnston, Jackson, and Polk Counties. And what about that clearing where we found you, Elton? With all those burn marks, weird yellow sand, and everything flattened but you? And, hey, we all saw the light."

Sheriff Peabody's face and body language grew increasingly uncomfortable as the deputy built his case. The department had way too many pots on its stove to make room for some UFO inquiry. Drugs, school gangs, the still unsolved Clem Edwards murder case, and a slew of other matters were already piled high on the department's plate, and he had a reelection fight in just a few weeks. He could easily imagine all the potential press interest in a UFO investigation, as well as his reelection opponent—fired long-time Deputy Sheriff Ray Campbell—getting great mileage out of the whole affair. Indeed, he knew Campbell to be deeply embittered and completely capable of charging his former boss with diverting the department down some UFO space hole and, following the lead of his own brother, to the neglect of local crime concerns.

Bo was also very worried about his brother's mental stability and with it the emotional health of the whole family. Twelve years back, when Elton had a nervous collapse, he was admitted to a psychiatric hospital out of state. It had been a terrible strain for everyone, not just out of concern for their loved one, but also to keep it secret. Cleburne was a friendly town full of fine folks, but there were still taboos and the family had enough to address without answering questions about Elton's mental health. If his brother was having another emotional break, Bo wanted it contained in the family. It was his desire that this entire lights drama become a distant bump in the rearview mirror as fast as possible. What good would it do anyone to investigate a UFO anyway? It could hold the whole department up to ridicule and further strain his brother's nerves.

"Let's not speculate, Otis. We don't know what it was. But the swell news is nobody was hurt. And it's all past tense now. So, Elton, let's get you home."

Bo drove to their parents' house, a two-hundred-acre farm on the edge of Cleburne. He had no intention of letting his brother stay the rest of the night alone at his own place. Nor did he want to wake his wife Stevie and the girls by taking him home. And he did not feel like babysitting him at the department while his deputies drove all over the county scouring the skies for some alien invasion. *Lord only knows what kinds of rumors are racing all over creation by now,* he thought.

When they woke up the parents, the first thing their mother remarked upon was her elder son's sunburn. Not only had his face suddenly gotten pink, but so had his arms and hands—even the palms. Bo had not mentioned it, not wanting to further alarm his brother. Elton had interpreted the deputies' long glances at him as signs they questioned his sanity. Too tired to take in his mother's concern, Elton went right to bed in the room he and Bo shared growing up.

Bo told their parents what happened. They listened without a word. No one acknowledged it, but there was an unspoken understanding it was circle the family wagons time. They would deal with this as methodically as they had faced Elton's collapse many years before. The doctors had warned them he was to avoid any extreme stress since that could precipitate another breakdown. Hence, his decision to forgo a PhD program and teach at his old high school near family, friends, and acquaintances. The family resolved to do all it could to protect Elton.

CHAPTER 3

Sheriff Peabody's fantasy that the whole matter would quickly evaporate was shattered by the lead story in the next morning's *Johnston County Gazette*. Below the headline, "BIZARRE UFO LIGHTS SHOCK LOCALS," an unusually long article breathlessly recounted the previous night's events, with quotes from several citizens who had called the Sheriff's Department to report seeing a strange light or lights on the county's west side. Bo raced through the story at his office desk, hoping there would be no mention of his brother. But there was. While mercifully not on the front page, two paragraphs were nevertheless devoted to "Johnston High School history teacher Elton Peabody" for having had "the closest encounter with one of the lights." Furthermore, "Mr. Peabody was reportedly quite shaken by the experience."

Bo winced at the description, resigned that the affair was now out of his hands. He angrily wondered who leaked the information about his brother. He had pointedly told "the UFO posse"—as the paper now christened the group of deputies and "concerned citizens chasing the purported UFO in the woods"—to not speak to the press. But only the deputies were obliged to obey him, and he did not want to guess who may have talked to that cute new, and single, reporter who penned the story, Kenley Kitchens. What a shame several of his deputies still weren't hitched, he lamented.

21

Glancing at the wall clock and seeing it was 8:00 a.m., he quickly turned on the Cleburne radio station, WCNE, to get the news. After the national reports, he was surprised when the first local story focused on a Johnston County zoning dispute. He was further comforted when the second addressed Revival Week at several area churches. And he exhaled deeply when the third brought up the pressing issue of whether it was an appropriate use of tax dollars for Cleburne citizens to call 911 requesting the fire department rescue their cats from trees.

But just as he reached to turn off the radio with relief, the news reader, Ophelia Turner, excitedly announced: "But by far the biggest story to hit this area in quite a spell concerns all the UFO sightings last night in Polk, Jackson, and Johnston Counties. In fact, the heaviest concentration and the most dramatic events occurred right here in Johnston County not far west of Cleburne."

Sheriff Peabody groaned loudly enough for his secretary, Casandra Leonard, to ask if he wanted his morning coffee. She figured he was dragging a bit when he failed to make his usual pit stop at the coffee and donuts table en route to his office. She had also rarely seen him reading the paper as he entered the building.

"No, shug. I'm fine. Thanks."

He knew he hit a home run hiring Miss Cassie. She was everything he wanted in a secretary: efficient, kind, friendly, intuitive, and absolutely trustworthy. She was also charming, made folks feel welcome, and had even won the local Miss Blueberry Contest, having entered it on a dare for laughs. She came from a fine family and had helped with the sheriff's election campaign four years before when she was still a high school senior. She supported him because he was the brother of her favorite teacher and, after years of having an old sheriff who once gave her a ticket when she was just five miles over the speed limit, she cottoned quite well to the notion of having a new one under thirty.

Bo had been so impressed by the girl's enthusiasm, willingness to work, and wit that he hired her as soon as he took office. So she worked for him during the day and took classes at Stonewall Jackson Community College in the evenings. Yet she still made time to come in some on weekends when the department was especially busy, like this Saturday morning. The truth was she enjoyed being at what she called "the center of where it all goes down in Johnston County" and would howl in laughter regaling her most trusted friends with the juiciest stories from the Sheriff's Department. She was the one who got to type up and file away all the sheriff's reports.

Now listening to the radio with new intensity, Bo heard Miss Ophelia go into far more detail about last night's UFOs than was typical for local stories and at much greater length. A slew of Cleburne folks were happily quoted about various types of light they saw in the sky, woods, and behind Billy Ray's Rib Shack. Even the Jackson County High School Rebels' tennis team reported a brilliant white light following its two vans as the players returned home from a match at Johnston High. The large, radiant light had followed the team at tree-top level for several miles along the winding highway. After the news segment ended and Sheriff Peabody again started to silence the radio, local radio personalities Mason T. Phillips and Tammy Jean Robards came on the air. They were hosting a special Saturday edition of their weekday morning call-in show to "discuss and analyze the big local UFO controversy." Sheriff Peabody leaned back in his swivel chair, gripped a pen behind it, and stared at the ceiling. It was already shaping up to be one heck of a spectacular Saturday.

The first caller was Ned Thurston, the town's long-time leading conspiracy theorist. Bo and his deputies had been to his farm more than once to investigate Mr. Ned's claims that his cattle were being slowly and deliberately poisoned by radiation leaked from a nuclear power plant. When the sheriff and Deputy Hill pointed out the nearest such plant was two states away, Thurston countered how that just proved the leak was a malicious effort to destroy cattle out of state. When the sheriff asked why the in-state cattle would not be even more vulnerable to any leaked radiation, Ned retorted they had been immunized against it. When A.P. pointed out his own sister lived on a farm near that very plant and had never told him any such thing, Thurston trumped him with the "inside information" it was an undercover state government operation. Secrecy was the whole point. Now Thurston was convinced Johnston County was facing a potential alien invasion.

"Mason, Tammy Jean. Now y'all are making all sunshine and strawberries about this here UFO business. But I'm telling you, we need to take this thing as serious as cancer. With all the UFOs that was seen last night—and most of 'em right here in Johnston County—that is no coincidence. And this notion that UFOs are always peaceful just ain't true. There are loads of cases where they are hostile. I'm talking alien abductions, sometimes with women even being violated. If you're familiar with UFO research like I am"—Bo had no doubt of that—"then you know we need to be on guard and armed and vigilant at all times."

Bo put his chin in his hand and stared out the window. But the tall magnolia tree he liked to gaze upon was overtaken by visions of citizens patrolling neighborhoods with shotguns aimed at the heavens.

The next caller, "Azalea from Cleburne," he recognized as Azalea Knox, a sister congregant at First Presbyterian Church. She claimed to have seen three UFOs the night before and volunteered they appeared to be on a scouting mission for further exploration and possible colonization. She became the first witness to claim to have seen striking details of their craft, including multicolored metal and search lights inspecting her neighborhood, especially her home. Sheriff Peabody recalled Deputy Cummings's report from last year documenting Miss Azalea's claims of being visited at home by emissaries from "Satan's Air Force." Otis had gently asked if she was on any medication and was told she had recently run out of her "nerve pills." The deputy called Dr. Parish to call in a refill which Otis picked up from the pharmacy for her that evening. That had been eight months back. The sheriff wondered if she needed another refill.

Back at the family home, Mrs. Peabody was fixing breakfast for her husband, Joshua; Elton; and Melody, Elton's twenty-five-year-old sister. She was a middle school teacher who had come down from the mountains for the weekend to visit their parents. She too had been apprised of the previous evening's events in hushed tones by her mother while Elton slept.

To his surprise, he had finally, mercifully fallen asleep a few hours before daybreak. He was also relieved he had not shook during the night. He did not know if it was due to his being with his family, shock, exhaustion, or all three.

Any hopes it had all been an atrocious nightmare collapsed when he saw himself in the bathroom mirror that morning. To his amazement, his face, neck, arms, and hands were quite sunburned. He had gone from near jet-white to pink in one night. *This should go over real well at school on Monday*, he mused. How would he explain it to the students?

The rest of the family was instantly cheerful when Elton arrived at the kitchen table. He immediately recalled that same forced positivity many years before when he had last been in crisis. But he was grateful and returned a forced smile and "Good morning." He also noted how the morning paper was not on the table. He could easily guess why.

Joshua and Ruth Peabody were life-long residents of Johnston County whose families had lived in the area since well before the War Between the States. They lived on the same farm that had been in Joshua's family for three generations. While Mr. Peabody farmed, Mrs. Peabody taught fifth grade. Both were Sunday school teachers at First Presbyterian Church. They were hard workers who were grateful to have reared three children who shared their values.

Since no one else would bring up the events of the previous evening, Elton decided to take advantage of the lack of shakes and get it over with now. So he recounted the same story shared with Bo and Otis. When he finished, his mother asked if he felt all right. His father and Melody quickly chimed in that there were many reports of UFOs the night before. It comforted Elton enormously that his family was supporting him unconditionally. He started to thank them but stopped when he felt he might cry. His mother smiled and took his hand, which made her elder son struggle even more to restrain his emotions.

His father spoke for the family when he declared, "Elton, your mother and I, Bo, and Melody appreciate what a terrible ordeal you've been through. But it's over, son. There's no reason to worry anymore. You've got nothing to fear. So let's just all get back to our lives. And you know you're always welcome to stay here as long as you like."

While gratified, it hit Elton that today likely marked the start of the rest of his life. He knew the previous night's drama would always be with him, others would identify him with it, and he would have to deal with it. Even if the lights never returned, the experience was in him and always would be.

After breakfast, his mother insisted on applying a cream to help his sunburn and hopefully ease the burning and itching that now accompanied it. Then his father drove him back to his house. Nothing was said of "the incident" as Elton now labeled it. When awkward silences arose, Mr. Peabody soon brought up topics of mutual interest. His son tried to maintain the conversation but was too distracted to hold up his end. So his father spoke of farm matters, about which he could talk endlessly. Elton appreciated his father's efforts and was grateful for the lack of silence.

When he opened his front door, General Longstreet leapt on him. For the first time since the incident, Elton broke into a grin. His concern that his dog might treat him differently was replaced with relief. After putting his mother's packed lunch in the refrigerator, he let Longstreet out the back sliding glass door. To his delight, the general raced outside. Apparently nature's call outweighed any unease about the previous evening. There was no barking now, from either his dog or those of his neighbors. Elton clung to the hope that life was blessedly back to normal.

He forced himself to venture into the backyard, refusing to cower before his fears. The hospital doctors and nurses had told him that avoiding them would only make them bigger. He looked at the woods for a long time, determined not to be intimidated. Contrary to his previous concern, they looked more peaceful and benign than he could recall. *You can't hurt me,* he resolved. *I won't let you.*

Since Longstreet was eager to play, Elton smiled again and had fun throwing a tennis ball for him to fetch. He marveled at the dog's complete immersion in whatever he did and with total enthusiasm. How wonderful it would be to have that natural ability or develop such a skill.

Back in the house, time passed slowly. He did not want to ponder his encounter, but it was all he could think about. He was grateful to turn on lights without any shakes, but there was just not enough to distract him. He tried reading the latest Napoleon biography but could not concentrate. Turning on the TV, he navigated through all one hundred channels but found nothing compelling. To combat his general unease, he put on a Bach record of strings and flutes. But his leg could not keep still, and he felt constrained. So he shifted to a Led Zeppelin album and cranked up the volume to try to drown out his anxiety. That did not work either.

So he ate an early lunch and decided he needed to get out. Besides, it had been a while since he had taken Longstreet to the nearby John B. Hood Park, and he was indebted to his dog for being such an island of cheer in a sea of stress. It struck him that the general was the one being who had not treated him differently since the incident.

As expected, Longstreet was elated to head to the park, eagerly inspecting everyone and everything in his path as they made the mile trek on foot. Elton wondered if he would see anyone he knew who had read the morning paper. He had sniffed it out after breakfast when his family was not looking and was more resigned than upset to be mentioned in the lead article. He had to acknowledge it was fair but dreaded what folks would think and ask him. To his relief, he and Longstreet had much of the park to themselves, and he recognized that he felt better when exercising.

Returning from the park, despite the risk of encountering acquaintances wanting to ask about the article or at least his sunburn (and what would he say?), he made himself run errands—anything to stay busy and keep the unfocused anxiety at bay. He recalled the advice of the hospital staff more and more: keep active, go out, see people, do things, stay busy to keep from obsessing about fears, but do not run away from them. Instead, confront them. Yet he also recalled them telling him to avoid stressful situations. Indeed, they were distinctly cool to his starting a PhD program. The pressures of earning a master's degree had prompted his mental meltdown. *Just get through the day,* he told himself. *One step at a time. Focus on stuff outside myself. It will get better. It always has.*

After running several errands, he had not been back at his house long before his mother and Melody surprised him with dinner. They had prepared one of his favorite meals and he reminded himself how blessed he was to have such a supportive family. Several of his friends did not. His mother wanted to know what he had been up to and was delighted to learn of his going to the park before running errands. She lingered a little at the door when leaving and stressed how he was always welcome to spend the night at home again.

He resumed his battle with Napoleon that evening and was able to read a fair amount of the biography, though not with his usual immersion in the material. Reading had always been one of the few pursuits enabling him to completely escape without risk. He took comfort that he was able to leave the incident behind him on many pages.

When it was time for bed, he caught himself looking at the sliding glass door curtains and noted the lack of any light shining through. He breathed a somewhat relaxed sigh as he walked Longstreet outside one last time that day and faced the woods at night. He made note of the lack of any lights, hum, or dogs barking. He also relished the sounds of crickets and owls. *Just dwell on how much better tonight will be than last night. In fact, think how much better every night will be*, he desperately hoped.

When approaching the bed, he noticed butterflies in his stomach. Looking out the window, he reminded himself there was no light. And then he tried to pray. He had been too exhausted last night to think of anything but the incident and tried to focus on nothing to forget it. But now he desperately wanted to make sense of his experience. He thanked God profusely for saving him from any physical harm and for his loving family and dog, as well as for helping him get through this first day of the rest of his life. Yet he yearned for understanding. The thought of going on and never learning what had really happened struck him as an appalling scenario, like starting a swell adventure novel and then suddenly losing the book halfway through it and finding out there was no other copy. He did not deserve this. Did he? Should he become a dedicated UFO buff devouring literature on the subject and researching everything he could about his own encounter? That was the last thing he wanted.

His earlier enthusiasm for the topic was no longer even a faint blip on his radar screen.

Unable to sleep, he called Longstreet. The dog liked to sleep in the den. If he needed to go outside, he would scratch on the sliding glass door until Elton let him out. As soon as he heard his name called, the general trotted into the bedroom. Elton petted him on the floor and laid back down but with his arm hanging beside the bed nestled in his friend's fur. How grateful he was to have finally heeded the advice of friends and gotten his dog. Sleep came at last.

He was appreciative to have slept more than the night before and with no nightmares. Now it was time to decide whether to attend Sunday worship services. He was reared in the church and, while never enjoying the solid faith of his parents, he wanted to believe in a loving God, especially when he was most anxious. He had several friends in the church and also did not want to disappoint his parents. And the Rev. Charles Presseau had been very good to him and his family when he was hospitalized. But did he truly want to face all those people this morning? Most everyone would have read about him in yesterday's paper and heard who knew what kinds of rumors. If not, they would surely notice his pink tan which was already starting to peel, and he had yet to decide how to explain that. He contemplated taking Longstreet fishing at the family pond instead, but did not want the family to catch him playing hooky and figured the quiet waiting for a fish to bite would not distract him enough; plus, he had just asked God to please help him get through this. Besides, he liked Dr. Isaac "Slim" Patterson's Sunday school class and was friendly with everyone in it. A few had left kind phone messages that weekend, but he had not felt up to replying. Now he could. So he went.

Before entering the building, parishioners welcomed him warmly. Today he found small talk much easier, and he was glad no one brought up the incident. His friends and acquaintances in Dr. Patterson's "twenties and thirties" class treated him the same as ever. They all acted normally, albeit a couple of ladies greeted him with a hug for the first time. No one at or after the church service brought up the incident either. His whole family lit up in smiles when he joined them in the pew. Bo even hugged him too, and his wife Stevie and their young daughters, Sarah and Esther, were especially glad to see him for the first time since last Sunday. And his mother said his skin was already looking better. What most stood out to him about the service was when, during a prayer, the Rev. Presseau asked God to comfort those who were confused, did not understand, could not explain, and felt lonely and afraid. Elton wondered if this was meant for him. *But it could apply to everyone at times,* he thought. Still, it sure felt like it was aimed his way, and he was moved.

After the service, in the receiving line, the minister took his hand with both his own, something he had not done since Elton returned from the hospital all those years ago.

"Hello, Elton. I'm so glad to see you. I still hear ever more compliments about your teaching, young fellow. And, hey, your daddy keeps telling me about y'all's fine fishing hole at the farm. How's about you and I going fishing there sometime?"

Elton said that would be swell and then joined the rest of his family at the home place for Sunday dinner. Everyone was upbeat and no one mentioned the incident. Bo sat by his brother and tried to watch him as closely as possible without being noticed. On the drive back to his house, Elton reflected on how well the church experience had gone. No one had asked about Friday night, nor were there any uncomfortable silences or anyone talking nervously around him.

He also realized that, despite yesterday's big newspaper story, no one talked of local UFO reports in his presence and not a soul mentioned his obvious sunburn. While grateful at how kind everyone was, it was obvious folks were reluctant to be fully themselves around him. How long would this continue? Had word leaked out all those years back about his going in the hospital and not being able to handle heavy stress? He tried to concentrate on how well-intentioned his fellow congregants were and just be grateful.

Back at his house were more phone messages, but this time from reporters and not just from the *Johnston County Gazette*'s Kenley Kitchens. Much larger papers from out of town, as well as TV and radio stations, wanted an exclusive interview about "your UFO experience." *Lovely. Now what?* he mused.

His gut told him not to return a single call. He wanted this entire affair to disappear like a snowflake on a hot stove. Talk to one journalist and a slew of others will call once another article about him appears. Look what's already happened this weekend after just that local story mentioned him, and without even an interview. The more articles about him, the deeper this incident will be scarred into his public identity. This could even cause serious trouble at school. What if "the UFO teacher" becomes a joke? He was dreading classes the next day and was braced for any number of comments from some of the show-offs he taught. Seriously, his job could ultimately be jeopardized. How about that for more anxiety? His mind raced to imagine himself having to move to another county to teach where no one knew him, only for the UFO stigma to eventually brand him there too.

Yet part of him was eager to confront the whole issue to hopefully get it behind him sooner. What if he just gave one interview to a really serious reporter who would write a thorough and fair piece explaining exactly what happened? Find someone well versed in scholarly UFO literature (did such exist?). Besides, he had done nothing wrong. He broke no law. Where was the shame in his actions? He was perhaps the only person brave enough to get close to that Godfrey Daniel light—or maybe the only one foolish enough. Whatever the case, he did not want to think about it. At least not yet. See how things go at school tomorrow and throughout the week. Maybe this will go away much faster than he feared. And recall how sweet everyone was at church today. Where he taught had a slightly different clientele.

CHAPTER 4

He would find out how different the next morning. Initially all seemed the same at Johnston County High School. Principal Robert Toombs greeted him warmly. They had always gotten on well. In fact, Elton was grateful to him for not only providing his first full-time job but complimenting him on his strong evaluations and working late, as well as awarding him several merit pay raises. Some faculty did not care for Mr. Toombs. Several secular ones thought he was too traditional for maintaining the annual Christmas choir concert and not only allowing student religious clubs but frequently attending their meetings. This confirmed Elton's suspicion that so many atheists just take religion way too seriously. Like Mr. Peabody, the principal always wore a suit and tie and urged the teachers and staff to dress more formally than those of other schools in the area. Elton did not care much for his detractors and could easily imagine what they thought of his own formal wear at work, as well as his advising the Presbyterian Club.

Other administrators and colleagues were all their usual friendly selves, at least the majority who were normally pleasant. The cold paper-pushers and bitter teachers who did not want to be there ignored his hellos as usual. Over a decade in the educational trenches had convinced him the ultimate four-letter word for the teachers and staffers who complained the most was "work." But they treated him no worse today. The first person to bring up the incident was Luke Frazier. He was a forty-ish psychology instructor who Elton had always cherished as a hard-working, fine teacher who was eternally cheerful.

"Hey, man. How's it going? I read about you in the local paper Saturday. What a weekend you must have had, eh? Not exactly a typical Elton Peabody Friday night, I imagine, at least not according to the *Gazette*. So what happened? Do you think you really saw a UFO up close? What an amazing experience."

"Ah, it was certainly nothing I want to repeat. I just followed this eerie light in the woods behind my house and then it just got super intense and loud and all around me. It was initially white but then had flashes of several other colors too. And then I guess it just all became too much, and I sort of blacked out. Then the cops arrived, and that was it."

"Wow. Are you all right? I see you're sunburned. But it looks like it's peeling. So that's good."

"Yeah, I'm okay. I just wish it hadn't happened. I'm sort of dreading my first class."

"Tell me if you hear any good UFO jokes," Luke laughed. "Gotta run. Take care."

Mr. Peabody arrived in his classroom early to prepare for the first lecture, a twelfth grade Western Civilization class. Since he covered the French Revolution last week, today he would give them a biography of Napoleon Bonaparte. He wrote all the major points he wanted the students to recall on the board and organized the show-and-tell items he would pass around to try to personalize and three-dimensionalize his subject: large images of the general, Elton's photo album from his trip to Paris that included pictures of Napoleon's Tomb, and his Bonaparte biographies. Having taught for over a decade, he long ago learned such items could excite more interest in lecture topics among the better students and often preoccupy others inclined to cut up or sleep.

It was with a mix of dread and excitement that he anticipated meeting his students. He braced himself for who knew what kind of rude, as well as innocent but still awkward comments and queries.

But he was also eager to dive into the deepest depths of the place where he could face the most ridicule. For all his frustrations with constipated educrats telling teachers how to teach (just imagine their reaction if teachers dared tell them how to administrate, he thought), occasionally difficult students (and a few parents), and some cold colleagues, Mr. Peabody relished teaching and did not know how to fill his life without it. So he was determined to take a proactive approach and try to hit a home run.

Ready for his first lecture, he left the classroom to use the bathroom, check his office mail, and avoid having to repeatedly answer questions about Friday night as the students arrived before class. He adored his students—most of them—and worked hard to create a strong rapport with each. In return for giving enthusiastic lectures in which he impersonated historical figures, his pupils—most of them—gave him their generally rapt attention and gratitude for not having to sit through another PowerPoint slideshow "lecture" in the dark read verbatim by a burned out excuse for a teacher. Still, these were fourteen- to eighteen-year-olds who were often not nearly as mature as they (and he) wanted to believe.

When he entered his classroom, he could feel a different energy level. Sure, many students ignored him, but many others looked at him with smiles and wonder in their eyes. There were a few chuckles as well as looks of concern. He also noticed someone had used green chalk to draw an alien on the board with a caption saying, "Give us back Mr. Peabody."

"How was your weekend, Mr. Peabody?" asked Prudence Ashworth. "Anything special happen?" Prudence was a cheerleader who sat on the front row, was a solid A student, and was a poster girl for the ideal pupil in many ways. She was always in class, on time, taking lots of notes, positive, and acing the tests and papers. What she lacked in originality she matched in cheerful dependability. So Elton was grateful her well-intentioned question was the first.

"I bring you all greetings from the Planet Wild Rumors," he proclaimed to raucous laughter. It was the kind of explosive chortle that was also an expression of relief.

"Unfortunately, its spaceship was so brightly lit and with such a loud hum that I couldn't see or hear any of its emissaries. Perhaps they were too intimidated by the powerful physique of Earth's representative or put to shame by his incredibly good looks," he added.

The class was roaring now, so much so that old Miss Gertrude Nast pressed her face against the long classroom window facing the hall, first surveying the class before squinting and staring at Mr. Peabody. She had never approved of the popular history teacher. Indeed, she did not care for lecturers showing excitement, passion, or humor in class, and failed to see why any instructor ever needed to leave the lectern. When Elton greeted her in the halls, she looked away or flashed the briefest smile. At sixty-nine, plus a lot of tax, she could have retired with a pension many years, if not decades, ago. But she had no husband or any children that she knew of, hobbies, known friends, or much else aside from her passion for boring science students with lectures not updated in decades. As he had done before whenever she walked by and was inspired by laughter to pointedly stare at the culprit, Elton gave her his biggest grin and waved, prompting her to immediately leave. *At least one mission accomplished.* He smiled.

This was not so bad, he thought. In fact, he was enormously relieved. But before he could start exploring the life of the French emperor, a satisfied Penelope Breen interrupted. She had been his student in various classes for four years and a prominent presence in all of them. Yes, Miss Breen was a bright show-off and thrill-seeker who was easily bored, but Mr. Peabody was grateful for her willingness to ask provocative questions about historical figures no one else dared pose or perhaps even think of, like whether the American Revolution was really justified, or if President Lincoln deserved assassination for his brutality to the South and unconstitutional actions, or—most infuriating to many classmates—if all religions were mere fairy tales. She coveted creating controversy and did not care who she upset, unless he was a cute jock.

However, due to some of her conduct after class, Elton studiously maintained a bit of an aloof remove from her. Yet that may have only attracted her to him more. Because he was one of the few faculty whose classes did not bore her, she would ask more questions about historical figures who intrigued her after class. Except she did not stop there. She pushed for information about Mr. Peabody's dating history and whether he would ever take out a student, especially a senior who was already eighteen. Combined with her promiscuous reputation, this made him hesitate to be seen by colleagues talking with her in the halls where she liked to walk alongside him (and a tad too closely) and loudly ask personal questions or make risqué comments in the presence of educrats. She especially relished asking a sexual question as Miss Nast walked by one day.

Very attractive and flagrantly flirtatious, she emphasized her well-developed figure with tight-fitting, low-cut attire. Indeed, on several occasions Principal Toombs had talked to her about this, twice even sending her home to change with a note to her parents. Penelope got a lot of male attention but took extra pleasure in embarrassing boys too shy to approach her, especially if she had an audience. Before her tenth grade World History class one morning, Elton saw her sit on the desk of the quietest boy in the room to play with his hair. Too scared to say anything or even move, he just sat and sweated. Mr. Peabody quickly told her that was enough and to sit at her own desk. Another time he heard her call across the room to another shy boy, hold up a screw, and ask, "Hey, Ernie. Wanna screw?" Most students rolled their eyes, several grinned, the boy became watermelon red, and Mr. Peabody promptly told Miss Breen to turn around.

Her particular brand of cartoonishly coquettish immaturity isolated her from most of the girls who saw her as an exceptionally bad girl. To them she was a rude, selfish narcissist who saw everyone as a mere prop for her amusement. Her notorious purported sexploits, which she enjoyed shocking people with, had sealed her reputation with the bulk of female students and more than a few males. But many boys were taken with her beauty and the fact she was a rare pretty girl who deigned to approach, talk with, and compliment them like few others in their lives. The flirting did not hurt, either.

But despite all the talk—much of it her own—she never had a known boyfriend, at least not at school. With the exception of the prom and a few other big school dances, she had rarely even been seen out on a date. When a star football player she went out with once bragged they had had sex, she not only exposed his lie but ridiculed him in public to the point where he secretly went to the guidance counselor's office and sobbed. All but a few boys were too intimidated to ask her out. She claimed they were way too "immature" and, besides, she preferred "college men."

So Elton was skeptical of her sexual prowess. Despite her swagger, he saw a remarkably smart, intuitive, and creative girl who was undisciplined, quite insecure, and very lonely. Since she had almost no boundaries when talking with him, he learned her father had long been absent from her life. And in the four classes he had taught her, not once did her mother attend the annual parent-teacher night when mothers and fathers would meet each of their children's instructors. Penelope had little to say about her, and nothing positive.

It was obvious she treasured her talks with Mr. Peabody. Indeed, at times she had come to his room to talk during the lunch hour and after school. Such occasions always prompted Elton to make sure the door was wide open and the room's blinds all the way up, facing both the hallway and the courtyard. Once, while eating lunch at his desk, she tried to sit on it but was immediately told to take a seat behind another.

Still, Elton enjoyed talking with her. He had to admit she was one of the most unique, intellectually talented, and intriguing students he had taught in his ten-plus-year career. In class, it was students like her who helped everyone examine what might otherwise be ignored. She got him to share a lot of information and ideas he otherwise would not have, and often the most memorable statements in the entire lecture. She was also adept at creating class discussions, which were sometimes not wanted by the instructor when he was inevitably behind in his lessons.

He also enjoyed her uninhibited talk outside of class since, there as well, she dared to challenge him in ways others would not. And they had many thoughtful conversations about interpersonal behavior. He believed her frank observations gave him more insight into the delicate, sometimes still mysterious, psyches of adolescents. He identified with her loneliness and wanted to help her, as he did with every student. That he spent time outside of class talking with and (especially) listening to students without casting judgments made his classroom a magnet for students out of the mainstream. Elton well remembered how alone and particularly fragile he felt in high school and tried to be the mentor at school he never had.

That he found Miss Breen quite fetching, both in looks and demeanor, was a source of amusement and worry. Though he valued his career and reputation far too much to entertain ever going out with her, he felt guilty having fantasized about her, especially before she turned eighteen. While his heart told him maybe they could go out a few years after she graduated, his head knew that would be a Pandora's box of guaranteed regrets. But she still enjoyed taunting him.

"You know, I'm really attracted to older guys," she once confided after school with a sly smile, to which Mr. Peabody rolled his eyes and snorted, "Um, hmm."

"I am!" She laughed. "So what if you asked me out sometime?"

"Sure, why shouldn't I destroy my career? What's to lose?"

"So who would ever know?" she cooed.

"Gee, I don't know. Everyone."

"All right, what if we wait until I graduate?"

"Oh, sure. Who in the world would have a problem with a man in his mid-thirties going out with a teenaged former student young enough to be his daughter? Who could possibly object? Just your parents and virtually the entire community."

"My parents don't know who I go out with and don't care. You think I give a flip about my father? Where's he been my whole life? Or Mom, so stuck on her work and latest boyfriend? She wouldn't even notice."

"What makes you think I'd even want to go out with you?

"No!" She laughed. "Then how come you spend so much time talking to me and about personal stuff and all?"

"How can I avoid you? You keep coming here when I'm captive eating lunch or trying to do work after classes. Some folks might even say Miss Penelope is stalking poor Mr. Peabody."

At that, she squealed and laughed and, for the first time, appeared to blush. While she thought of her history teacher as only moderately good-looking, there was no one else in her life who not only would not let her intimidate him but could crack her up with a wry wit, even with her as the target.

So it was with trepidation that Mr. Peabody now turned to the infamous Miss Breen on this morning he had dreaded more than any he could recall. Though tempted to ignore her and anyone else with unwanted questions, he concluded it would be better to confront all their curiosity and embarrassing comments now and hopefully be done with them.

Taking her time to achieve maximum attention and pausing at times to stifle a chuckle, Penelope confidently asserted, "Well, I heard you went *inside* that UFO, Mr. Peabody, and the authorities are covering it up. It's another government UFO conspiracy. You wouldn't have any connections in the Sheriff's Department, would you?"

Laughter ensued, along with a chorus of *wooh*s. Elton's soaring spirits sank. This would not go away with a few jokes. Reality had intruded again.

"No, ma'am. Reports of my having anything like that kind of a 'close encounter' are so vastly exaggerated as to be pure fiction. As a history teacher, I deal in facts. Now y'all know I love science fiction—you've heard my references to Ray Bradbury's *Fahrenheit 451*, Robert Heinlein, Philip K. Dick, and others. I've mentioned how *Close Encounters of the Third Kind* is one of my favorite films. So if I really had some 'Mr. Peabody Parties with the Aliens' tale to tell"— more loud guffaws—"I assure you I'd be telling my story to all the press, in addition to y'all. But have you seen me give one interview?"

"But maybe that just proves the conspiracy, that you're hiding something." Penelope smiled and looked back at the rest of the class. A chorus of uh-huhs rang out.

"And I think somebody may be standing on the edge of the diving board, saying, 'Look. Look at me, everybody. See me embarrass Mr. Peabody.' It won't work, dear."

Her grin burst into a laugh amplified by several more students. To the shouted additional questions, Elton raised his hand and announced he had nothing further to say about the matter.

"Look. I know y'all are curious, and I would be too. But I don't have anything more to add to what the *Gazette* said Saturday about my following a light in the woods and…finding it was incredibly bright and loud, and that was it. Yes, it was scary and no, I don't know what it was. If I did, I would tell y'all and the whole wide world. So that's it, and we're now moving forward to discuss Monsieur Bonaparte."

A spate of groans was followed by a question for which he was not prepared. Gil Roberts was his least favorite student that year. He was a loner who made a fetish out of trying to shock others with his studied cynicism and snide remarks belittling every purported hero discussed in class. It appeared his greatest goal was to disillusion everyone. All but a couple of other misanthropes ignored him, but Elton had tried to be extra nice to him "to whip a man with kindness," as Granddaddy Alonza Peabody had taught him long before. But Mr. Roberts was immune to such decency and apparently received it so infrequently as to not know how to handle it. He remained obnoxiously determined to provoke.

"Since you have so few details about this *encounter* with the big, bad light, and don't want to talk about it, then how do we know anything even happened at all?" he asked.

A sudden silence descended awkwardly over the class, accompanied by several angry clucks. Sorely tempted to snap at him, Mr. Peabody reminded himself this was an angry, miserable boy half his age who wanted his teacher to lose his temper, and in front of the whole class. *So do not give this jerk that satisfaction,* he thought.

"That's right, Mr. Gil, I just made the whole thing up, along with all the other dozens of witnesses in three counties calling the law about it Friday night. Yep, and most of the Johnston County Sheriff's Department just suddenly up and decided to go roast marshmallows with me in the middle of the woods that evening…and your humble history teacher was the one lucky enough to get this gorgeous pink tan for apparently sitting too close to the fire. Alas, while y'all have tan skin and white teeth, Mr. Peabody has white skin and tan teeth… that is, until Friday when his skin went from jet-white to jet-pink. And while everyone else sunburns during the day, I do so at night and in March. So, sure. That's right, it's all just one massive conspiracy. Don't all the pieces fit just perfectly?"

The students laughed again, and there was even some applause. None liked Gil and, as usual, he had tried to undercut whatever was the prevailing story. Elton was relieved to have refrained from sharing what he really thought of the insinuation and was touched that, despite the inevitable questions, the students seemed solidly on his side. He still felt sorry for Gil and a little guilty for politely but pointedly putting him down in front of the class. But that snide meanie had earned it, he decided. Richly.

It was finally Napoleon's time where the class remained until the bell sounded to end the first period. To Mr. Peabody's relief, the students appeared to pay close attention to him, ask some good questions, laugh at all the right times, and enjoy the Bonaparte souvenirs (especially the photo album—his pupils particularly enjoyed looking at pictures of places they had never been and of Mr. Peabody not wearing a suit and tie).

The pattern stuck for the rest of his classes that day: nervous walking into the classroom, greeted by a variety of applause, it's-UFO-man-type statements, and supposed spacecraft noises (especially with the ninth and tenth graders), followed by the same questions and answers, and then the lecture. Each class got easier and less tense and, based on what garnered the most laughs, he honed his answers for maximum merriment. His plan was to keep it all as light as possible with him being the comic ringmaster and hopefully (most) everyone laughing with and not at him. And to his surprise, he was able to concentrate reasonably well on the subject matter.

But its application worked better in the classroom where he was more in command than anywhere else. In the halls he noticed several students he did not know grinning and pointing at him, and a few made sci-fi movie soundtrack noises walking by him. He smiled and waved. *Don't let them intimidate me,* he told himself. *Make this as weightless as cotton candy. Don't run away. Don't be any bully's bull's eye.*

The faculty who brought up the incident were friendly and concerned, at least most of them. A couple of the ones who rarely spoke to him appeared to take special delight in making fun of the matter, especially when he checked his mail in the teacher's lounge. He just smiled, answered as vaguely as possible, and said the press and rumor factories were vastly exaggerating the whole affair. Long ago he came to see the faculty lounge as a haven for the laziest and biggest complainers, as well as a snake pit of gossip about colleagues not there.

After his last class adjourned, he sat at his classroom desk to rewind the day. Each lecture was reviewed for what worked and what did not, and notes were added to lesson plans accordingly. The next day's lectures were studied with notes made for how much material he would hopefully cover (but rarely would due to fun stories, questions, and discussion). He then thought back on each class to determine whether there were any students who appeared to be having trouble, academically or personally. Mental notes were made to call on this student in class or try to converse with that one afterward, perhaps have a conference with this one, or even think about talking to the school's guidance counselor about how to help that other one.

To be frank, the day had not gone badly at all. If anything, he wanted to believe his UFO encounter had made him somehow more personable to his students. Lo and behold, Mr. Peabody actually had a life outside of history class and it was not a complete bore. The students had seemed to be on his side about the matter. No one charged him with outright making the whole thing up, and you had to be color blind to not notice his premature hot pink tan in March. It had been quite touching when a few students stopped by during his lunch hour to ask if he was okay. He was grateful and wanted to believe his reputation for hard work, dependability, and honesty was successfully sailing him through some rough currents that might otherwise overtake him.

But just as he was feeling the best about the matter yet, his least favorite educrat made a special visit to his classroom. Over the years Elton had seen so many ambitious assistant principals and other bureaucrats try to impose their brands on the school. While a few had been decent and competent, so many wanted to tell the teachers how to teach and were determined to burden instructors and students alike with endless new and wholly unnecessary paperwork.

Teaching over a decade had taught him too many educrats were obsessed with power, prestige, and rigid rules. Education and the welfare of students meant nothing to them. Indeed, he learned in his first year teaching that the bulk of educrats appeared most interested in money and numbers, and the latter was but a means to the former. How well students did on arbitrary, often politically corrupted, standardized tests trumped any actual learning or critical thinking. Getting better scores on state exams to get more federal, state, and local tax dollars—and by most any means necessary—trumped any real education. He regarded most of the lot as a class of professional leeches constantly looking for ways to justify their jobs and usually at the expense of teacher autonomy and student learning.

"Elton, I'd like a word with you," said Frank Sneed, the assistant principal in charge of discipline. To Elton's ears, the words sounded like barks from a thoroughly constipated Rottweiler. It was as though a surprisingly cheerful dream had just been shattered by an especially shrill alarm. He also noted how, typical with this speaker, there was no "hello," "please," or "thank you." Reality intrudes again. He sighed.

Mr. Sneed personified so much of what Elton had resisted his whole life. The wiry, balding forty-year-old was a bureaucrat on steroids, a man who liked imposing endless new rules on students and loved enforcing them without mercy. Many faculty felt he betrayed a particular penchant for rooting out any instructors who might not scrupulously adhere to his diktats. Elton had heard "the Warden" (as most students and many teachers called him) was forced on Principal Toombs four years ago after a series of student misbehavior incidents at the school got leaked to the local paper and radio station to embarrass the county superintendent of schools and the rest of the educrats at the Johnston County Board of Education. Plus the elected school board members had gotten some complaints from parents which prompted them to put pressure on the superintendent to impose a tough new disciplinarian on the school. Enter Frank Sneed.

Though Elton acknowledged the school had had fewer behavioral problems during Sneed's reign as Johnston High's minister of the interior, he thought this had been achieved at the cost of instilling unnecessary fear in too many students, especially shy ones like he had been who were not hurting anyone. Indeed, what good came from suspending a freshman or sophomore—and for a whole week—just for leaving campus for lunch? Who benefitted by requiring students to have a note from a teacher, educrat, or staffer to walk down a hall during class time? Such neurotic orders smacked far more of a prison than a school, Elton contended. And God help the child who dared to smoke behind the gym, under the stadium bleachers, or anywhere else on campus, for Mr. Sneed was a nico-Nazi who could smell smoke within one hundred yards.

How much more regimented the school had become since Elton walked these halls twenty years before. He wondered if fearless Frank had ever had a tough time as an adolescent and speculated how much more frightening his own high school experience would have been with such a self-important bad clown patrolling the halls.

While Mr. Peabody and Mr. Sneed had never had a direct argument, they were certainly not on each other's Christmas card list. On several occasions Elton had intervened on behalf of students he thought were either being punished for something ridiculous or punished too much for something minor. While he lost most such cases, occasionally Principal Bob Toombs overrode Mr. Sneed. Elton figured Bob wanted to be his ally in all such cases but was under tremendous pressure from the superintendent, the county educrats, and the school board to look like he was on board with their tough disciplinary regimen.

So rather than answer him, Elton just smiled at Mr. Sneed and remained seated, pen still in hand and body leaning over his lessons. He had little doubt what this was about and could well imagine how Friday's incident could easily be twisted into fodder for Sneedy purposes.

"Now about this alleged UFO matter, Elton. Now I don't know what happened, or what you may think happened over the weekend…and I don't want to know and don't care. But I do care passionately about the welfare of this school, and this is exactly the kind of thing Johnston High does not need. I've already heard students in the halls talking about you and whatever happened over the weekend. Well, we can't afford to have students whipped up into some kind of little green alien hysteria distracting us from our mission, and with the annual state tests coming up soon too. And we sure don't want any teacher becoming known as 'that UFO guy.' I don't think you want that, either, Elton. So I think it's in your own interest to downplay this whole matter. And remember, you are a representative of this school and not just here on campus."

Elton's smile had grown ever more contemptuous throughout the practiced pitch. *The nerve of this five-star jerk,* he thought. *I have done nothing but teach five fine classes today despite a lot of pressure, and this is the thanks and support I get?*

"Thanks for your concern, Frank. But everything went fine today. My classes were consumed with Napoleon Bonaparte, Andrew Jackson, and the Vietnam War, with just a brief cameo appearance of a 'little green alien' at the start of each class, and only in response to a few questions. The students, faculty, staff, and Principal Toombs have all been quite supportive of me." He wondered how long he could maintain his smile.

"Well, let's see to it that's the way it stays," Mr. Sneed warned. "I've got more than enough on my plate now than to have to deal with any kind of 'UFO' problem."

"Why would you have to deal with any *UFO problem*, Frank, especially when the only person I've encountered in this whole school today who's tried to make it a *problem* is you?"

Now Mr. Sneed paused, lifted his head, and squinted at Elton. For the first time since entering the room, he was no longer in fifth gear but had come to a total stop. Mr. Peabody's smile remained.

"Let me tell you something, Elton. I'm wise to your passive-aggressive attitude about discipline on this campus. It's obvious you try to undermine my efforts to maintain a proper educational environment here. You don't fool me. Yet I still decided to do you a favor today by warning you of the very real potential danger to your career if you don't handle this foolishness well. Well, now you've been warned, buddy. I am watching you and will not hesitate to bring you down if your presence here becomes the least bit detrimental to this school."

Elton had become livid. The person in front of him now embodied every bully with an imperialist personality he had ever encountered. A flash of angry memories featuring each official thug with whom he had ever dealt flew across his mind. *How dare this loser deliberately try to ruin my day, and totally unprovoked too.* His Christian upbringing and conscience told him to "turn the other cheek, judge not lest ye be judged, love thy neighbor, and do unto others as you would have them do unto you." *Well,* he rationalized, *if I ever act like such a colossal ass to somebody, this is exactly how I want him to do unto me.*

There was a silence that neither was sure he wanted to break. But then Mr. Peabody thought he detected just the slightest sliver of a smile start to dimple Mr. Sneed's face. The die was cast.

"Got your erection, Frank?"

For a couple of seconds, Frank Sneed's face was a stone. Then his eyes blinked. Twice. His nostrils flared. And Elton Peabody's former smile was now a full grin. Though he knew his antagonist could make his life more stressful, he also knew he had tenure and likely a lot more support than Mr. Sneed, and his study of history taught him appeasement never works with bullies. So the grin remained.

With his hands now on Elton's desk, Sneed slowly snarled, "The nerve of you, Peabody. Care to explain yourself?"

"Glad to, Sneed. After all that masturbation about how much you love the school, I figure even you might have gotten a little wood by now." Grin intact.

"Peabody, I'm going to have your ass," the assistant principal practically spit.

"Well, Sneed, that's all I'd ever give you," Peabody replied. Grin still intact.

Sneed stared at him for several seconds before quickly leaving the room. For a good thirty seconds Elton's stomach muscles were quite tight, and a mild case of the shakes gripped him for a couple of minutes. But the longer he sat and reviewed what Frank had said to him, the more justified he felt in his replies. He had only summoned the courage to stand up to bullies a few times in his thirty-five years, but each time he had felt so much better. This time felt best of all, and the grin returned. He fondly recalled something his late paternal great-grandfather, Artemis Peabody, had told him more than once: "Son, a far better judge of your character than who your friends are is who are your enemies. And if you're doing right, you should be right proud of every one of them."

Still, should he talk with Principal Toombs about what just happened? Elton could easily see Frank making sure the Sneedy version would be the first he heard. But Bob had always been good to him, backing him every time a parent had charged Mr. Peabody with discussing too many controversial issues in class, allegedly spending too much time on the extracurricular activities of someone's favorite president, or daring to tolerate open discussions of words and opinions condemned as "hateful" and therefore verboten by those parents, educrats, and faculty who prided themselves as being the self-appointed commissars of all that was correct. Elton had long suspected folks who get so easily "offended" may desperately need to get laid. He also speculated they could use a strong laxative, likely "extra strength."

No. Don't add another layer to this drama. Bob would back me, he told himself. *I saw how typically kind Principal Toombs was to me this morning. If Captain Jerk makes a big deal out of this, fine. I'll defend myself with everything I've got, and I'll also do all I can to bring down that SOB. But I've got enough troubles to address without creating more,* he thought. *Focus on how far better this day went than I dreaded. Be grateful and drown in the positive.*

As ever, when he got home that evening, faithful General Longstreet was waiting excitedly. There was added joy this time since Elton had not felt this well since early Friday evening. So he played fetch the tennis ball with the general even before he heated up his mother's Sunday dinner leftovers.

He was also touched that his parents, brother, and sister called to check on him. No one mentioned the incident and the topics were the stuff of small talk, but everyone expressed noticeable relief when Elton assured them the school day went quite well. When he mentioned his unpleasant encounter of the Sneed kind to his mother—sans the off-color language—she made a point of reminding him how there was a long line of folks who would not attend the farewell party of "that rude man" whenever he thankfully left his post.

Elton finally returned the calls of friends who had left phone messages over the weekend to ask how he was doing. He was not yet ready to relive Friday's incident in conversation, but it was comforting that there were people who appeared to care more about his well-being than the details of a prominent local news story.

He did not return the calls of any of the growing number of reporters from papers in the tri-county area requesting interviews. While tempted to publicly tell his own account of what happened to hopefully dispel any phony rumors or exaggerations, he still wished the whole thing would just evaporate.

The next two days at school also went well. Not one class began with questions about the matter, and the number of students, staffers, teachers, and educrats looking differently at him in the halls was waning as well. Sure, there had been a few students making jokes at his expense, but nothing mean. So could he already be on the downhill slide of this rollercoaster, headed toward a smooth end? He did not need to remind himself how reality kept intruding at just such times, but he tried hard to dwell in the ever-improving present. Even his sunburn was getting better.

CHAPTER 5

Sheriff Beauregard Peabody had no desire to hit another lick at "the UFO matter." On Saturday he had given his handwritten report to Casandra to type and file with instructions to stamp "NOT URGENT" on it, which meant do nothing about it. She knew from his expression not to ask about it either and warned the rest of the department to leave him alone on this one.

Most colleagues heeded her advice. But not Deputies Otis Cummings and Rufus Pike. They had accompanied the sheriff on what the *Gazette* articles termed Friday night's "UFO hunt" and approached their boss Monday afternoon about continuing the investigation. Bolstered by all the local press coverage, they were persuaded beyond a reasonable doubt they and so many other folks in three counties had in fact seen a number of strange lights in the night sky, and about half their department clearly witnessed one settle in some woods on the west side of Cleburne before it suddenly disappeared. Furthermore, someone or something had completely flattened the whole clearing in the woods where the light had been and even left some burn marks on the grass. The sheriff's own brother had obviously been utterly spooked by something in that exact spot. And just that morning the Johnston High Chemistry Department's report analyzing the strange pale-yellow sand found at the site could not determine what it was. Sheriff Peabody knew all this as well as they did. So they asked if they could continue pursuing the case.

"No," the sheriff replied. "There's no victim and no crime, and we've got far too many real victims and real crimes to address. I appreciate y'all's interest, but we don't have the time or resources. Now, if this thing returns, then we'll deal with it then. Otherwise, it's over, boys. Y'all did a jam-up fine job Friday and Saturday on this thing, but it's time to move on."

That halted the department's UFO investigation, at least for Monday. Though his officers were disappointed, they respected the sheriff tremendously. He had hired most of the present deputies, including them, treated each like a friend as well as a mentor, secured a small pay raise for all of them in each of the last four years, and refused to fire them when they made rookie mistakes. They were young and appreciated they owed him a lot. They also knew Sheriff Peabody was facing what could be a rough party primary challenge in fifteen days from the one deputy he had fired, Ray Campbell, whom the deputies could not stand. Indeed, if Campbell won, they figured they might well soon lose their jobs.

They also knew Sheriff Peabody did not like a lot of public-ity unless he was confident where the newspaper stories were going. He was not like some sheriffs who regularly pitched scoops to local reporters so they could hopefully get their picture in the paper with some apprehended crook or just looking important. Though that was usually a smart strategy for reelection, this sheriff preferred a low-profile law enforcement presence.

Furthermore, the deputies knew how completely shaken up the sheriff's brother had looked and sounded Friday night, and they had never seen their boss so solicitous of anyone. Yes, he was scrupulously polite, professional, and attentive with everyone. Nor did he hesi-tate hugging a crying witness. But the deputies had not seen their leader look as worried as he had with his brother that evening. They knew the Peabody family was close and, though Elton was actually two years older, they sensed Bo played the role of the protective big brother. So they figured there were many reasons this investigation would not go forward without additional credible UFO sightings.

But credible or not, the newspapers and radio stations of Johnston, Polk, and Jackson Counties continued to run front-page stories about various UFO reports in their communities. Local radio shows were inundated with calls from residents wanting to share and discuss what they claimed to have seen that Friday night. Under pressure from a few county commissioners who were UFO buffs, the Polk and Jackson County Sheriff's Departments had already announced plans to further investigate "the local lights." Now many in Johnston County—all of them voters—wanted to know why there was no further inquiry into the lights spotted by so many in their own county, especially since *The Gazette* reported more UFO calls were logged by 911 operators in Johnston County than in the other two counties combined. And the only known instance of police officers getting out of their cars to try to track down a possible UFO on foot occurred in Johnston County—led by the sheriff himself who also helped interview the case's star witness.

Despite all the valid reasons why he was confident such an investigation would be a ridiculous waste of the department's limited manpower, time, and tax dollars, Bo knew the top two reasons why he had dragged his feet. First was his concern about the God-only-knows-how-fragile state of his brother's mental health and the impact another breakdown could have on their parents. They were twelve years older than when Elton's last breakdown occurred and starting to experience the inevitable health challenges of aging. As stressed out as Elton had been trying to write his master's degree thesis all those years back when he checked himself into that mental hospital, Bo had never seen his brother look anything like he did Friday. As hard as he had tried to not think about that these last few days, it remained his hulking shadow. Others detected something was preoccupying him. His wife Stevie noticed how much worse he slept over the weekend and how much more he snored when sleep finally arrived. When he brushed off her queries about whether anything was bothering him, she intuited there definitely was. She knew better, she told herself. After all, she had been married to him for just over a decade and had been his college sweetheart years before that.

Though Sheriff Peabody felt guilty admitting it even to himself, the unpredictable impact a potentially high-profile UFO investigation could have on his reelection in just over two weeks was another major concern. He knew he faced a potentially potent challenge from Ray Campbell. His former employee had been a deputy for twenty-one years and had never had a negative mark on his record before Bo became sheriff. In fact, Campbell had been the most popular deputy around the county for years. He appeared to do a good job by the public's lights and was extra popular with local children when he visited schools. Indeed, old Sheriff Speaky Stevens was so uncomfortable speaking in public—and especially to children since they were more likely to ask embarrassing questions—that for many years he had delegated most school presentations to his long-time top deputy, Campbell. Now many of those children were registered voters who were still incredulous as to why their much younger, less experienced new sheriff had dared fire the department's most visible face on the streets two years ago. Initially, all Sheriff Peabody would tell the press was that it was a private personal matter. When the public demanded more information, he said there had been a long record of unprofessional conduct that he would not reveal out of respect for Mr. Campbell and his family, as well as to get the matter behind the department as soon as possible.

Though Bo had hoped sparing Ray any more humiliation would be rewarded by grateful silence on the latter's part, that had not happened. Instead, the fired deputy had publicly complained about his sacking and criticized his former boss's leadership in the press, comparing him unfavorably with his long-time respected predecessor, Sheriff Stevens. His firing had shocked and deeply hurt Ray. Since Deputy Campbell had worked for the department ever since graduating from high school, it was the only full-time job he had ever held. He had long enjoyed dreams of becoming sheriff himself one day, though he shivered at the added scrutiny and additional workload (especially paperwork) the job would entail. Ray was now a car salesman who sorely missed being a big shot driving around the county in his squad car. So he never hesitated trashing the present sheriff and many of his deputies—he had never forgiven them for all standing by the new sheriff—to everyone who would listen.

Better spoken and looking than the incumbent sheriff, the flirty, charming challenger was waging an aggressive campaign, putting up posters all over the county with his picture (and in uniform, to the disgust of Sheriff Peabody) under the headline: "THE EXPERIENCE YOU CAN TRUST—AND JOHNSTON COUNTY NEEDS." While no polls were out, Bo was clued into the county's gossip well enough to know he could be in electoral trouble, and he had no doubt a refusal to sanction a UFO investigation was likely to prompt Ray to charge him with ignoring "the will of the people." He also figured his election foe would attack any UFO investigation as "a silly waste of the people's resources." Politics.

It galled Bo that Ray had been such a selfish jerk about his firing. He knew better than anyone what a compulsive womanizer he was, having slept with a sizable share of the female employees in the county courthouse and propositioned many more. He had caused a lot of feminine heartbreak and nearly broken up a few families, and Bo thought he was incredibly blessed to have avoided a sexual harassment complaint or even a lawsuit. That Ray had a wife and three daughters and was a deacon at the First Baptist Church just galled him all the more.

While Bo had enjoyed working under Sheriff Stevens's leadership, his biggest disappointment with the old man was his looking the other way for years regarding Ray's unprofessional conduct. Bo was convinced his predecessor's long-time friendship with Ray's father was a major factor. That Ray Sr. had earlier worked as a deputy with Sheriff Stevens, and their families socialized together and went to the same church just aggravated matters further. The more he thought about it, the angrier he got at what he saw as Ray Jr.'s complete narcissism.

Bo smiled at the memory of Cassie telling him when Ray hit on her. The deputy suddenly sat on her desk outside Bo's office—when the sheriff was out—and offered to take her in his squad car on a tour of Loveland, a local lovers' lane at the far end of the county that was a dirt road around a pond hidden by woods. He told her they could "investigate the area and see if anything comes up."

Imitating Mae West with a Southern drawl, his intended prey cooed, "Well, that would be just darling, Deputy Campbell. And this

Sunday morning I can tell Mrs. Campbell all about it in her Sunday school class she's been after me to attend. In fact, I do believe your generous offer just convinced me to become the newest addition to her 'Young Singles' group. Now your wife and I will just have *so* much to talk about."

While proud she was no gossip—and, if anyone had the goods to spread, it was her—Miss Leonard told the sheriff every word of her exchange with Deputy Campbell. Bo had been methodically keeping an off-the-books file on his playboy deputy (typed by Cassie) and was waiting for just the right incident to fire him. Ever confident, Ray had finally met his romantic Waterloo.

On the immediate front, and contrary to the sheriff's fervent hope and efforts, "the local UFOs" may have physically left Johnston County last Friday, but they had planted all kinds of psychic seeds among many locals, especially in the press, that were already bearing fruit rich in gossip. While Bo hoped the lack of a story in Sunday's *Gazette* meant the event would soon fade from the local radar, Monday's edition had another front-page story with more details about "the strange lights" seen in three local counties. The ambitious new young reporter, Kenley Kitchens, was again the author. On Tuesday, her lead story exposed the lab results revealing local chemists had "no idea what the strange yellowish sand found at the main UFO site was." With each new article, ever more concerned citizens had come forward to tell the tales of what they saw of "the Friday night UFOs." Though the energetic Miss Kitchens left repeated messages on Elton's answer machine imploring him for an interview, he had not returned her calls, hoping the story would die much quicker that way. He was fine with getting recognized for helping students or teaching honors, but not this. Plus, he did not know the reporter and that mattered in Cleburne.

All the growing press focus had led a slew of constituents to call the Sheriff's Department to ask for or even demand *a full investigation* of the matter. Several congregants at church Sunday urged Bo to do so and, by Tuesday, folks were even calling his home. On Wednesday alone, Casandra logged no less than seventeen calls requesting an investigation.

That afternoon, Cleburne Mayor Buddy Simpson dropped by the sheriff's office to complain of so many voters calling him, city councilmen, and county commissioners wanting to know why Sheriff Peabody was refusing to investigate the matter further, as reported in Monday's *Gazette* and on WCNE Radio. The fifty-three-year-old had been Cleburne's mayor for eight years and came from one of the most prominent families in Johnston County. His father had been mayor, an uncle was the pastor of the largest Methodist Church in town, his brother was a former county commissioner, and his wife was the president of the local chapter of the United Daughters of the Confederacy.

"Come on, Bo. We're not saying you stage anything like a full-scale operation on this thing, just enough so we can say the county's looking into it. Give that *Gazette* reporter an interview, talk a good game about all the different angles y'all are pursuin' with it, and then let this thing fade away. By saying no investigation—especially when Jackson and Polk Counties are already looking into it—we look bad, man. And it was *your* Sheriff's Department that went into the woods after that thing—not the city police—so y'all should take the lead on this," the mayor pleaded.

"And spend the *county's* money on a wild interstellar goose chase instead of the city's," Bo chuckled. He and Buddy had always gotten along well, and he understood the pressure the mayor was under, all the more so since he was in a reelection fight too. But Bo recoiled from the political pressures of the job and tried to avoid the department doing things for political purposes, especially if the public was misled in the process.

"Bo, you're still new at this game. And though I know you want to think of yourself only as a lawman, you are every bit as much a politician as I am or you better be if you want to keep this job. And I'm telling you, you could very well lose reelection over this stupid UFO mess. I've been in politics a heck of a lot longer than you have, and this kind of thing is serious. When this many voters are calling their elected local leaders about something, those officials ignore it at their peril. Miss Cassie told me she's already logged over *fifty* calls about this since Saturday...and don't get angry at her 'cause I asked her. Now I've said my piece, and it's your call. But I hope you're not stubborn about this."

"Buddy, I appreciate your concern, your take on this, and your advice, and I promise to think about it. Hard. There are just so many factors, and I don't want this to sidetrack us from our primary duties. I really believe this department is doing a jam-up good job now. It's been real hard work getting us to where I think we ought to be, and it's just such a frustrating, ridiculous distraction to have to fool with any of this. You and I know nothing's going to come of it. Heck, if the feds still can't confirm any UFOs are manned by little green men from Planet Who-Knows-Where, how in the world is Johnston County going to prove anything?"

Smiling, the mayor stuck out his hand. "You're doing a swell job, Bo, and I want you to keep it."

They shook hands, the mayor left, and then the sheriff told Casandra to hold all calls but emergencies as he shut the door. He was resigned to having to make a tough decision and sensed what it would need to be. He knew the mayor was right in practical political terms and, despite all the endless pressures, late nights working, and struggles to spend enough time with the wife and girls, he knew he loved his job. He had dreamed of being sheriff since he was a boy and had lived his life toward that aim. As unnecessary as an extended UFO hunt would surely be, he realized he would have to do something in that direction or risk losing reelection, and he was certain the people of Johnston County would be significantly less well protected by Sheriff Ray Campbell.

Yes, it might be unpleasant for Elton to endure more interviews, but he's a thirty-five-year-old man who's done rather well since his breakdown twelve whole years ago, he reminded himself. Besides, Elton told him things were going fine at school this week. His brother would get through this, and it was not fair to the county for the sheriff to let family considerations trump the desires of his constituents, he reasoned. If he wanted to keep his job and continue helping the locals, he needed to reopen the investigation (albeit keep it limited) and just be extra gentle with Elton. The family would help on that front too, he tried to reassure himself.

Sheriff Peabody rarely visited his brother during the week, generally seeing him at weekend family get-togethers and church. But he wanted to tell Elton in person about his decision to reopen the investigation before it soon hit the local press or, likely even sooner, the Cleburne gossip express. Not wanting to dare see him at school since that would jumpstart all kinds of rumors, he waited until after supper Wednesday evening to stop by his brother's house.

Elton knew something important was up, or his brother would not be on his front doorstep on a weeknight. When Bo's face lit up into a big open-mouthed smile to greet him, he was certain the news was bad. General Longstreet's enthusiastic greeting to the contrary, Elton braced for full impact once they sat in the den. After Bo was reassured his brother's students and colleagues had treated him well that week, he got to why he was there.

With a long sigh, he faced his brother. "Elton, I wanted you to hear from me that I'm going to reopen the department's investigation of the…these U…the light or lights we all saw Friday night. It's not something I like, not even a little bit. I think it'll be a total waste of time and tax money. But too many locals want it. They're calling me, the commissioners, city councilmen, and the mayor. And I guess you've seen all the articles in the *Gazette*. Lord, that new gal reporter over there is as tight on this thing as a tick on a hound dog."

"She's left three phone messages."

"Well, don't answer them. I'll talk to her. Don't let her pressure you, Elton. Or anybody else. I don't want to reopen this mess, but the public's demanding it. Good Lord, it's probably the most exciting thing that's happened here in a real long time for a whole lot of folks. The fact that Jackson and Polk Counties have launched investigations just puts all the more pressure on us to follow suit. I'm sorry, man. This ain't how I wanted it. I had Miss Cassie file Friday night's report in File 13, which means ignore it. I'm sorry. But I promise we'll try to just interview you one more time, and I'll do everything I can to see to it this whole thing is kept as low profile as possible. I really think that's the best way for it to just fade away. Once the public knows we're looking into it, folks will back off, gradually forget about it, and then find something else to get fired up about. But I'm sorry I couldn't contain it, Elton."

"I know. I know," Elton assured him. "I understand and I can only imagine the pressure you and all the local officials are under. I get it and I don't blame you, Bo. You've got nothing to apologize for. I do appreciate all you've done for me about this. I really do. Thanks a lot."

"Are you okay?"

"I've been getting better. It's still not back to the way things were Friday afternoon, but I'm getting through it."

"You can always call any time. And you know that goes for Momma, Daddy, and Melody too. And… I'm sure Rev. Presseau would be glad to talk with too, if you want."

"I know. You're right. And I'm grateful. Many thanks."

Bo patted his brother on the back as he left. He felt better than when he arrived and told himself they would all ride this out after all.

"Well, boy." Elton looked at his dog. "Life might just get a little bit rockier. How I wish you could give me your eternal optimism and good cheer."

CHAPTER

It was later than usual before Elton got to sleep that night. The questions he had tried to suppress by going into full workaholic mode just would not leave him. What *was* that incredible light Friday? Who or what sent it? Why was he apparently the only person to have had such a disturbingly close encounter with whatever it was? What did it all mean? What was it that compelled him to doggedly venture into the light? Had it, or they, chosen him? Would it or they return? And if this was some kind of religious experience, why did he feel nothing of the kind? But how would he even know what such an experience felt like? As often as he had prayed to have just one, he never had.

Long after midnight, sleep finally found him. But it was not the kind he wanted. At one point he saw himself in the same clearing facing that ferocious light with the hum roaring. Only this time he angrily marched right into it. To his shock, an army of Assistant Principal Frank Sneeds marched out from a giant spacecraft. Each one was bearing a laser weapon aimed at Elton. It was then he realized this was a nightmare, albeit with a comic twist, and he ran charging into Sneed's Army and awoke. Initially angry, he had to laugh at the absurd irony.

Thursday morning's *Gazette* announced the Johnston County Sheriff's Department had officially reopened its UFO investigation. Sheriff Beauregard Peabody was quoted as stating, "This was a significant event in the life of our county and, while frightening to some and exciting to others, a great many folks want to know what actually happened. That is what this department is committed to finding out to the best of its ability."

But Miss Kitchens' story went on to note the sheriff stressed how "this effort will in no way be allowed to compromise any of the important progress we've made on the drugs, gangs, and other crime fronts." Elton knew his brother well enough to understand how much actual effort was likely to be expended on the matter. He owed him.

Each Thursday afternoon after classes was when the Presbyterian Club met. Early in his career, when the club's previous long-time faculty adviser, Virginia Carswell, retired, Principal Toombs asked Elton to sponsor the group. Bob knew he was Presbyterian and thought a much younger teacher would be a positive change for the students. That he was male could hopefully inspire more boys to join the girl-dominated group as well. So Elton had reluctantly taken on the responsibility. While this would look good on his annual self-evaluation, especially with his very religious principal, Elton questioned if he had enough conviction for the gig. He envied his parents' deep faith but had never felt anything like their certitude. He wanted to believe and went through the motions but was never remotely sure. Still, he liked his Sunday school teacher, Dr. Isaac "Slim" Patterson, and his minister, the Rev. Charlie Presseau, and had several friends at First Presbyterian Church. Far more significantly, his family was there every Sunday and then had a big meal together at the farm. It just did not make sense to break a lifetime's worth of tradition with good people, the dearest to him in the world. And he deeply respected his parents' quiet, unobtrusive brand of religion. Indeed, he had long believed a single, soft-spoken Christian setting a positive example did far more good than all the pompous, preachy, professional "Christian" hypocrites combined. No self-righteous zealot had ever changed his mind about anything.

Most importantly, he needed God too much. He had found the only thing more frightening than the prospect of a harsh, judgmental God was a life without any God. When his intellectual skepticism about the existence of God and his bitterness at enduring troubles had generated periods where he did not pray, he felt a loss of meaning and purpose. And a desperate loneliness. He had never felt more alone than in that out-of-state mental hospital. But perhaps his nightly prayers had helped him through that and a lot more since. They did not appear to have harmed him any since last Friday either. Indeed, with the exception of the pink burn that was already almost gone, he had not been harmed.

Over the years Elton had come to enjoy the club ever more. Its students were among the school's sweetest and smartest, and he already knew most from church and his classes. He enjoyed getting to meet the rest. There was never any behavior problem, and he liked getting a chance to be something of a de facto Sunday school teacher. Though he found much of the Bible hard to believe, he was fascinated by its history and treasured getting to discuss it and the moral questions it raised in far more depth and frankness than he could in his class lectures due to US Supreme Court rulings stipulating strictly secular instruction in public schools.

Plus, he had yet to feel comfortable enough to offer to teach a Sunday school class. Most of the other such teachers at church were much older and sure looked like true believers. With all his doubts, he felt like he might be an imposter who could easily become too controversial if he was ever too honest with his questions and frank discussion. What if someone complained to the director of Christian Education or even the Rev. Presseau? How embarrassing that would be for the whole family. But with the Presbyterian Club in the public high school, and with teens eager to explore and discuss their own questions, he felt far more at ease. The rebel in him also relished resisting some ardently secular teachers' mumblings about trying to get rid of all the religious clubs on campus. The proud Presbyterian in him wanted at least one Christian club on campus that was an alternative to the far more fundamentalist Baptist Club. And he was delighted with all the worthy philanthropic projects the Presbyterian students had spearheaded over the years.

Each club meeting began with a reading of scripture chosen by a member, based on whose turn it was in the student rotation.

Club President Elasiah Edmonds selected today's Bible reading. Her mother gave her a feminine version of the prophet Elijah's name, and Elasiah was the first black president of the club and a favorite of Mr. Peabody for always being so kind and cheerful. He was relieved she was a junior who would hopefully get reelected as club president in the fall.

"Let us listen to the Word of God from the book of Joshua, chapter 1, verse 9, in the King James Bible," she announced. "Have not I commanded thee? Be strong and of a good courage; be not afraid, neither be thou dismayed: for the LORD thy God *is* with thee whithersoever thou goest," she read.

This was followed by Vice President Daniel Franklin's opening prayer. He was the group's first male officer in years, and Elton was pleased the tenth grader had joined the club soon after Mr. Peabody mentioned in class one day that he was its adviser. Elton knew the stigma a boy would endure as a member of such a club among some of his unchurched peers, and admired the boy's not only staying in the group but getting elected as an officer. Elton was ashamed he had been too concerned with classmates' opinions to join the club when he was a student.

"Dear Lord," Daniel began, "we thank thee for this beautiful spring day and for our living in a country where we can freely worship you. Thank you for all the many blessings you've given us, and please help us remember to give thanks for them and do good and be strong and have faith in you. In Christ's name we pray, Amen."

Club business ensued with reports from various members heading up efforts to better promote the club around school, collect more cans of food for the local poor, tutor students who were struggling academically, and spread the faith. Then it was time for the members to talk about whatever they wanted: a particular Bible scripture or story that moved or confused them, a prayer request, a problem or conflict they wanted spiritual advice and support for, or concerns about the school or issues concerning the nation and world at large.

Mr. Peabody encouraged the students to develop their own leadership skills. But he was quick to take the reins if the members were shy or unsure. He found assisting the students with their problems and trying to bring spiritual comfort to them—often just listening sympathetically—appeared to genuinely help them. It also made him feel better.

Today the first question concerned whether Mr. Peabody was comfortable sharing his recent experience with the now (in) famous local lights and whether he thought the hand of God might be involved. Someone mentioned the purported UFO experience found in the Old Testament's book of Ezekiel, and another asked if he thought the light he encountered came from angels.

Elton was touched by how gentle and concerned the students were. Outside of his family and closest friends, he believed he could find no friendlier, more supportive group with whom to confide. So he decided to be completely candid. When the students eagerly confirmed they would like to hear the full story, he told them, but without any of the shaking or sweating that accompanied his initial interview on the subject. The students sat in rapt silence. Two girls wiped a tear when he conveyed how terrified he had been and fervently he had prayed. When he finished the account, he confessed he could not say what or who was behind any of it. He doubted it was religious in nature, not wanting to believe God would frighten him so and without a clear explanation. This led to a general discussion of what UFOs might be, and Elton was relieved at how relaxed he was. In fact, he felt comforted being surrounded by several folks who clearly supported him. A couple of the students suggested he talk with the Rev. Presseau about it all. He answered he would consider that.

When it was time for the closing prayer, he was surprised and quite touched that Naomi Taylor at one point asked God to watch over Mr. Peabody and help him not be afraid of his recent encounter, helping him understand and take comfort in the Lord. As he felt himself at risk of tears, Elton bit his tongue and tried to think of something else while the mantra of "Do not cry" kept repeating in his head. When the students all repeated "Amen," he could not speak for a minute as the boys shook hands with him and the girls hugged him. Instead he smiled, nodded, and was grateful.

Walking back to his classroom, Elton tried not to think but just dwell in what felt like a protective warm glow of goodwill and even love. Thoughts of how foolish he was to worry so much enveloped him too. In recent years he had begun to believe his top regret was having fretted over so many fears that proved to be utterly unfounded or trivial. Wasting so much precious time worrying should have been his biggest fear, he concluded.

The halls suddenly appeared as vibrant kaleidoscopes of colors full of youthful energy and hope. It was as if he discovered himself in a delightful dream and did not want to think too hard or he might wake up. So he tried to focus on this newfound sense of well-being to delay reality's return as long as he could.

Upon entering his room, he saw Penelope Breen sitting on his desk reading his Bible. This was a sight that had never crossed his radar screen. Not wanting to pop the bubble, he froze and just took in the image with a growing grin.

"There you are," she smiled. "I've been waiting for you and wondering where you were."

"Each Thursday after school is when the Presbyterian Club meets. I'm the faculty adviser. We'd love for you to join us, Miss Breen. You'd be most welcome, dear."

"Um, I don't know. We might not be the same speed. But I bet they're real sweet. What do y'all do? Talk about God and stuff?"

"Yes. And pray, read the Bible, share each other's concerns and challenges, and work on projects to try to help the school and our community. We meet each Thursday at 3:30 in Room 212. Come join us. You might like it. Everyone will be kind to you and you won't be judged either. Elasiah Edmonds is our president this year. You know her. She's a very nice young lady."

"I don't think she likes me. I've seen how she looks at me sometimes when I sit down."

"Hmmm. It couldn't possibly be she's just surprised at some of the more provocative outfits Miss Penelope chooses to try to squeeze into to shock the school, now could it?"

"Mr. Peabody," she laughed. "How dare you. The other girls are just jealous I've got the guts...and the figure...to wear them."

"Is that what you waited patiently to enlighten me about?"

"No. I was just concerned about you. You haven't said anything about your recent bizarre experience since Monday, and I've just been thinking about you and wondering how you're doing. That's all."

For the first time in knowing her for the better part of four years, Elton actually felt touched by Penelope. Gone was the gossipy, flirty, teasing provocateur, and in her place was a sensitive and thoughtful young lady.

"That's mighty thoughtful of you, Penelope. I really appreciate it. Thank you. I'm all right." He sighed. "And this week has gone so much better at school than I could have hoped. I'm real touched by how decent everyone…almost everyone…has been about it. It's just so weird, disturbing, and confusing, and now the Sheriff's Department is reopening the investigation and more and more reporters are calling, and I just want it all to go away as fast as possible so I can get back to my old life."

"Aw." Penelope frowned and touched his arm. "I'm sorry. Hey, but just think how incredibly cool this is. I mean, I know it's tough now. But you'll get over it, and how many people ever have such a wild experience like you did? You could write a book about the whole thing and even get to go to UFO conventions. Yeah, just think. You could be there with all those sci-fi geeks dressed like space monsters, and there's Mr. Peabody, the most normal one of the bunch!"

"Honey, I assure you that is the last thing your humble history teacher wants. I really didn't struggle through graduate school to become 'the UFO instructor.'"

"Oh, but that would be *so* cool." She laughed. "All the students would want to take you. Well, they do now anyway since you're about the only teacher in this whole stupid school who's not a bore. You and Mr. McKenzie and Mr. Frazier and that's about it."

"Thank you, Penelope. I do appreciate that."

"Man, I'd love to have a UFO experience. It'd sure spice up my boring life. And from what I've read and heard, you actually walked *inside* that light and it was so intense you passed out or something. That's awesome."

"Rest assured it did not feel *awesome*. In fact, that's about the last word I'd use to describe it."

"Well, I think it's super cool." She laughed. "I'm so jealous. With half the county chasing UFOs everywhere, only Mr. Peabody has the brains to find it and the guts to walk right inside it. And then it's so intense he passes out. It sounds so… sexual: 'an extra close encounter of the *ultimate* kind.' Ohhh." She was now rocking with laughter.

"Miss Breen, this was most definitely no sexual experience. Sex was the last thing I was thinking of at the time. You're just being ridiculous. Here the one time I see Penelope Breen actually reading the Good Book, and then I'm so moved by what I take to be your heartfelt, genuine concern about the most frightening experience of my life, and dog if you don't find a way to turn it into some kind of bizarroland sex joke. I should have known."

She was now laughing too hard to stand and had to grab a desk to keep from falling. He just looked at her and shook his head. Wouldn't it be wonderful to be able to see the absurdity of it all and just laugh like her, he yearned.

"Such a silly gal," he remarked. But he was grateful she made him smile.

CHAPTER 7

Of all Elton's friends, the one he felt most comfortable with was Beryl McKenzie. Beryl taught English at the school and was Elton's closest colleague. A poet and confirmed bachelor in his late forties, Beryl lived across from Cleburne's largest cemetery in a little house dominated by many thousands of books, records, and a cornucopia of pop cultural kitsch. It was always a super swell smiler for Elton to visit. Indeed, he could and did spend hours talking with Beryl while wandering through the rooms and halls browsing his friend's enormous collection. They shared remarkably similar interests in history, literature, politics, culture, TV shows, music, movies, metaphysics, and even UFOs. Many a Friday and Saturday evening they had stayed up half the night trading ideas and speculations about joint concerns and curiosities.

Beryl had lived a far more experimental life in that he had hitchhiked around the country, taken a lot of hallucinogenic drugs, and lived with several women, experiences far removed from Elton's tightly bordered radar screen. The latter appreciated how eagerly Beryl shared so many fascinating, funny, and sometimes poignant tales from his younger, wilder days. Elton often urged him to write a memoir, but Beryl feared it would get him fired if ever published.

The students adored Mr. McKenzie for his passionate readings and uninhibited enthusiasm for exciting literature. Most were eager passengers on his animated lectures' journeys through a colorful literary landscape that included writers as variegated as William Blake and Aldous Huxley. They treasured just being in his classroom for all its funky posters of off-beat literary legends like Jack Kerouac and Richard Brautigan, as well as his pop music heroes, Ray Davies of the Kinks, Bob Dylan, and the Beatles' John Lennon. Mr. McKenzie's ponytail, tie-dyed t-shirts, and psychedelic bell-bottom pants distinguished him from the rest of the faculty, to Principal Toombs's frustration. He also wore buttons bearing witty literary quotes and images of novelists. Mr. McKenzie was an icon to students who felt isolated from the mainstream, especially aspiring artists. They were particularly impressed their English teacher had many poems and short stories published, some of which they had even read in class. How cool was that?

In addition to their many mutual interests, Elton and Beryl bonded for sharing similar emotional struggles. They were each other's one friend with whom they were at ease frankly discussing their shyness, insecurities, and brief stints in a mental hospital. Unlike with a shrink, family member, minister, or any other friend, Elton was able to confide in Beryl without fear of being judged or downgraded as a friend. That Beryl had notched so many more bohemian exploits than Elton ever dared also made it tough to ever shock his older buddy.

He appreciated how his friend had not asked what happened last Friday. Instead, Beryl left a note in Elton's school mailbox asking if he was doing all right. Beryl knew his friend well enough to know how shook up he must be and that he would share the experience when ready. He also treasured Elton as his closest mate and was grateful to have at least one friend in town with whom he could speak frankly on just about anything. So he was glad to let Elton unwind at his place after work Friday, and he knew what the main topic was likely to be.

When Elton arrived, it was as if nothing strange had ever happened. They shared notes about classes, what writing Beryl was doing, and recent books read and films seen by each. Then came a pause.

At last Elton asked, "Can I talk about what happened last Friday and get your take on it?"

"It's what I've been hoping for." Beryl smiled.

"It's just the most incredible experience I've ever had. For the first time it's as if I may have a tale to tell that might even rival some of yours," Elton mused.

"I think it may well eclipse all of them! From what I've read and heard, it's like a psychedelic drug experience, except in 3D." Beryl laughed, deliberately trying to keep things light since he knew, whenever Elton was pausing a lot, his pal was nervous.

At first slowly, especially when he felt he could cry, he told the entire story of the Friday night he would never forget. Beryl listened intently and never interrupted. It was after recounting all that occurred that unique evening when Elton started speaking much faster and more uninhibitedly.

"As intrigued by all those UFO articles and documentaries we've discussed where some guy or gal has the most remarkable encounter with what seems like an alien ship, a big part of me just never believed any of it was actually real. They had to be hallucinations or…something. But not real. Yet I didn't dream what happened to me…and I've still got some of my pink alien tan to prove it. I so wish it was all a dream or even a nightmare because no nightmare I've ever had can compare with this.

"And I'm not saying I saw some UFO. I don't know. That keeps dogging me, Beryl. I have no idea what it was. If I did, maybe I could get some closure on this thing and move on. Though, if it's shown it really was an alien encounter, then I guess my life becomes a fishbowl forever. Oh, dear Lord, please no.

"But it's just… I try not to think about it by working as intensely as I can and staying busy—reading, listening to music, watching TV, whatever. But it's so hard to concentrate, to get away from it. General Longstreet's never been happier because I've spent more time playing and walking with him this week than any time since he was a puppy. And he was scared Friday night too, but he got over it just fine. Not me. I just feel this constant, nagging unease following me everywhere. Yet folks have treated me really well…everybody but Frank Sneed."

"Well, he's the most constipated fool in the county."

"Right." Elton chuckled as Beryl winked. "But it's like you've been reading the most amazing novel or watching the most incredible movie of your life and you suddenly have to leave just before the big mystery is revealed. Yet you learn there are no more copies of the book or film, and nobody else has ever read or seen it. So you'll never know what happened. Except this is real life—my life—and it's as authentic as my sitting here talking to you. A big part of me feels like I can't go on without answers, but I just don't think there ever will be any. Yet the last thing I want is for that thing to come back and I really do find out what it is. I want it out of my life forever. For the first time in thirty years I wanted to sleep with the light on. At times I just want to crawl out of my skin. I feel so trapped and claustrophobic. Why did this happen? As much as I've fantasized about having an honest-to-God real UFO encounter—as much as I used to—I don't wish this on anyone. And why me? It's like my life has become some *Twilight Zone* TV episode about 'Be careful what you pray for, because you may get it.' So should I now be prepared for some twist where this light returns and it really is an alien UFO?

"And what if it's God in some form? That's what some of the Presbyterian Club students were asking yesterday. So should I be doing everything I can every waking hour to find out? Pray all the time? Talk with Rev. Presseau? But why would God try to send a message by terrifying me? And if it's got nothing to do with angels or religion, then why would He let this happen to me? Heck, us Presbyterians are supposed to believe in predestination. So why would God destine this to happen?

"I just don't know, Beryl. I don't know anything about it. I know exactly what happened and how I felt and feel now. But I've got no answers. None. There. That's it. I'm babbling now. So I should just shut up and hear your take, please. Thanks for your patience."

After a pause, Beryl replied, "I've been entranced, man. Thank you for sharing it all. I've got a front-row seat to maybe the most thrilling story in the history of Johnston County. And I'm honored you told me the whole thing. I've been thinking about it all week, and your revealing all this additional stuff has helped fine-tune my thoughts. So here they are.

"First, you'd be superman or God if you understood what really happened. So don't beat yourself up for not figuring it out. You'd have incredible extra sensory perception if you could. And my guess is, unless you have another encounter like this, you'll never learn what it was or why it happened. But you know what, Elton? That's okay. I know it feels terrible now, and I'd sure want to know all the answers too. But look at all the other folks we've read about and seen shows on TV about who had similar experiences. Yeah, they were scared and wanted answers. But they went on with their lives. And even though they never found out what it really was and almost none of them ever had another encounter...so don't worry...they went back to their normal lives like you already have and everything worked out.

"Remember, time is the great healer, and it takes time to get over anything tough. Man, when I lost Momma I thought I'd never recover. It took months before I got back to normal. And I still miss her and get powerful lonesome for her sometimes. I think of her at least once every day. Lordy, what I'd give if I could see or talk to her again.

"Don't forget you're stronger than you think, Elton. You got through your nervous breakdown and hospitalization. Is this as bad as that? Yeah, it took a while to get back up to speed, but you pulled through, got a job, and became one of the most popular, respected teachers in the school.

"I envy you. Don't take this wrong, but I'd love to have an experience like what you had last Friday. I could do without all the fear, and I'm sure I'd have been scared out of my mind too. But just think, man. You've had one of the most amazing experiences anybody has ever had anywhere. And you lived to tell about it and aren't even hurt. And you went right back to work and are doing fine. Yeah, you're shook up. You'd have to be crazy not to be. But you'll get through it. And now you've got the rest of your life to top everybody else's best story everywhere you go." He chuckled.

"Milk this thing for all you can, Elton! Once you get comfortable with it, you could write an article or even a book about it. Heck, we could watch Mr. Peabody get interviewed on TV on some UFO show. And just think of all the gals who would now love to go out

71

with Mr. Elton and hopefully hear all about his fantastic encounter with who knows what." He winked.

"I don't know about that." Elton tried to laugh. "But I appreciate your take on all this, and I do feel better. You're right that, as bad as it often is now, it's not nearly as bad as the breakdown. And I don't feel ashamed about this, like I've let anyone down. I did before. It's funny. With my breakdown, the family and I wanted to keep it all secret. And I think we did. This time everyone knows and a heap of folks want to know more. A slew of reporters have called to leave messages wanting interviews. But I'm just not ready to talk in public about it. I just tried to make light of it all with the students and make them laugh, which most of them did.

"Maybe I'm just feeling sorry for myself and having a pity party. Perhaps I should just man up, get on with my life, and be grateful I wasn't hurt, most everyone has been real understanding about it and, no matter how boring the rest of my life may be, I've always got this unbelievable story to tell. Although maybe, after a while, nobody will believe it. But then that could be a blessing too."

"It's okay," Beryl assured him. "You don't have to figure it all out. Nobody does. And it'll all work out. You're already over the worst of it. It should only get better from now on. Try to laugh about it as soon as you can. Go on with your life and lean on the folks you trust and who care about you. You can call me whenever you want. You know me. I'll never tire hearing and speculating about it."

Elton wanted to hug him but feared he would cry. So he just smiled and nodded. Beryl understood.

CHAPTER 8

After spending much of the night talking with his friend about his unique experience, as well as comparing notes on various historical and pop cultural topics, Elton enjoyed his best sleep in over a week. He no longer felt the need for the general to sleep by his bed and woke up Saturday morning feeling life seemed better than it had in a good while. So he did not hesitate to answer the phone when it rang after breakfast. It was the first time he had not screened a call in a week.

"Hello," he answered.

"Hi! Is this Elton Peabody?" asked an enthusiastic and hopeful feminine voice.

He suddenly realized she could be another reporter. But not wanting to hang up after such a cheerful and polite opening, he hesitated.

"Maybe," he replied. "Who's curious?"

"I'm Kenley Kitchens from *The Johnston County Gazette*. I've been investigating the strange lights last weekend, and I would be so honored and thrilled if you would please consider letting me interview you, sir, since I think you have information and insights that no one else does."

"I don't know." He sighed. "I don't want to become even more identified as 'that UFO guy' for the rest of my life. I'd just like this whole matter to disappear."

"Mr. Peabody, I hear you, and I don't blame you. I can only imagine what you've been through. But if you'll please let me interview you, I promise not to pressure you to answer anything you're not comfortable with, and I give you my word the last thing I want is to in any way embarrass you. I think you've had an incredible experience a lot of folks want to learn about, and I want you to know I'm totally on your side, sir."

He found himself becoming ever more relaxed as she talked. Hers was a slightly raspy yet still girlish voice he found distinctive, and she sounded genuine and heartfelt.

"You're saying all the right things, Miss Kitchens, and I'm tempted. Part of me would like to give the public my full account of what happened and be done with it. Perhaps that would reduce the number of ridiculous rumors and satisfy folks' curiosity for good. But it could also cement an image of me as some UFO loony tune. I appreciate your understanding, but I still don't know."

"Mr. Peabody, I appreciate your honesty, especially when you don't even know me. Maybe the best way I can hopefully convince you I'm in no way out to get you is to ask you to please read the other articles I've written about the lights. Have you gotten a chance to read any?"

He had. In fact, he had read all six, and each struck him as well written and entirely respectful of everyone who came forward to share what he saw that evening.

"I admire you, Mr. Peabody. You've had an unbelievable… I mean, amazing…experience, and I'm just fascinated as all get out with UFOs and any kind of mystery. And to get your first-hand take on all this would be the highlight of my career," she pleaded.

"You give me your word you'll do me fair?"

"Oh yes, sir. Absolutely. I promise."

"I may regret this for the rest of my life but, since you sound sincere and your stories have come across as fair to all and well written…all right." He sighed. "I'll give you an interview."

"Thank you! Oh, thank you ever so much, sir. I give you my word, you won't regret this."

"You're welcome," Elton replied. "I don't plan on giving another interview, at least not on this subject, unless you screw it up."

"I won't. Rest assured, I'll treat you right. Oh, thank you, Mr. Peabody, and I'll interview you whenever it's most convenient for you. You're welcome to stop by the *Gazette* office anytime or I could swing by the school, if you like."

"Thank you, but I don't cotton to folks seeing me at the *Gazette*. That might look like I'm running to y'all to tell my story. Nor am I wild about certain people possibly seeing me interviewed by a reporter at school about this." *Like Frank Sneed.* He shuddered.

"Would you like me to come to your place?"

He had not thought of that but did not like the idea of reporters learning where he lived.

"Or how about if we meet somewhere of your choice, where you'd be most comfortable? And someplace quiet where you'd have privacy," she suggested.

Since he planned on taking General Longstreet to Hood Park again that morning, he asked if she could meet him there. Kenley started to squeal she would love to, before restraining herself in the interest of professionalism. So they agreed to meet at one of the benches overlooking the lake in half an hour.

Once again, few folks were taking advantage of the tranquil little park that day, which was just kosher with Elton. Though he got to the bench a few minutes early, Miss Kitchens was already there with her notepad and tape recorder. At the sight of him approaching, she jumped up and stuck out her hand. As he took it, he marveled at possibly the happiest-looking smile he had ever seen. Time was suspended as he processed her presence. In fact, he could easily see himself becoming completely manipulated by her charm. She was taller and leaner than your typical American twenty-something, with such a clear, joyful face draped by long, black, straight hair and gorgeous green-gray-blue-hazel eyes. Her shirt was bright purple, and her pants looked like blue jeans except they were white. They also had paisley and flowers drawn all over them. When he remarked how impressive they looked, she boasted how she had drawn each one of them.

She endeared herself further with her affectionate greeting of General Longstreet. She shared how she had had dogs her whole life and loved them all. The general approved of her completely.

As they noted the pretty pond, Elton was further taken with her expressed fondness for fishing. She said she had moved to Cleburne just a few months back and asked where were the best fishing holes around and if he fished.

Could the *Gazette* have researched his likes and interests to come up with his ideal reporter? he mused. Best of all, she seemed to exude a *joie de vivre* that was absolutely enchanting. *But don't let her lull me into sharing anything I don't want to,* he warned himself. *I don't know this gal. Remember, she's new to town and may not have any loyalty to Johnston County folk.*

Only after he gave his permission did Kenley turn on the tape recorder and start the interview. She smiled and her eyes never left his. It was an effort for him not to feel hypnotized.

"First," she began, "what would you like to be asked about this experience? What is it you most want readers to know about what you've been through?"

Surprised but pleased, he answered, "I just want the record to show exactly what happened on the night in question regarding all the lights so many locals saw, and that includes my own story. I'd just like for the facts to be reported and then let people make of them whatever they wish. I don't claim to know what happened to me and may never know. If someone can enlighten me, that would be wonderful. But I'd like for this interview to help show precisely what did and did not happen to me that night."

"Great. I totally get it, and that's exactly my goal," she stated. "This article will do that."

Instead of asking a bunch of questions, she requested he convey his entire drama from that night, or as much as he cared to share, going at his own pace. Trusting her now, he relayed the whole story from the general's first frenzied barks right through to his interview with the sheriff. When he got to where he was facing the light up close, Kenley's smile had become open-mouthed wonder. When he slowly, softly relayed his trying to pray on his knees, she blinked often and he wondered if she might cry. Only when he finished did she speak again.

"That is the most awesome experience anyone has ever shared with me. Thank you, Mr. Peabody. Thank you so much, sir," she said quietly.

It was then she asked what he thought he might have seen and heard, how he was dealing with it, and what he hoped to finally get out of the experience. Thinking carefully and speaking slowly, Elton claimed to be open to the possibilities of some kind of secret, high-tech US military hardware, an elaborate prank, an alien spaceship, or something else.

Miss Kitchens never tried to move him in any direction. Instead, she queried him about whatever theory he was entertaining at the moment. When the interview was over, he acknowledged to himself that she was completely captivating. Why in the world had he not returned this remarkable gal's calls earlier? So, caught up in such a positive vibe and not wanting to potentially miss an exciting opportunity, he asked if she would like to get lunch after he took General Longstreet home.

She said she would be delighted. At his house, she was in awe of the large 1944 Japanese battle flag on his living room wall. A US Marine took it from an enemy soldier he killed outside Manila in the Philippines. Elton had bought it at an antique store before getting the Japanese soldier's handwriting on it translated and the flag framed. Then he showed her the backyard where his big drama began. Only after asking his permission did she photograph him standing with an exuberant General Longstreet in front of his backyard fence with the woods behind them.

Lunch was a dream. They went to the one eatery in town with a variety of vegetarian dishes, the Purple Thumb. Each was impressed the other enjoyed frequenting such a place. Once seated, it was his turn to play reporter, and she enjoyed telling him all about growing up in a small town that was a cousin of Cleburne. They had similar rural Protestant families, and she was excited to be in a new area as the paper's top reporter and finding the locals to be quite friendly and similar to those of her hometown. Elton had been the only person initially hesitant to talk with her. With her looks, but much more so her ebullient persona, he did not doubt that at all.

Though teaching had gotten him to become quite a performer in class and he had grown comfortable talking with most anyone, Elton remained very shy asking ladies out. But there was no way he was going to mess up this chance. Kenley was like that girl in a dream with whom you fell in love. When you awoke, you were too crushed to sleep for a while. But minutes before he was about to ask her out on a date, she mentioned her boyfriend back in her hometown. Reality returned.

But how wonderful he had met such a lovely lady with the most exhilarating vibe, he told himself. Unless her article was a betrayal of what she promised, he was confident he had made a real friend. To his surprise, when they said goodbye, she hugged him and flashed such a warm, gentle smile that he could only stammer thanks and goodbye. The rest of the day had a hazy hue, and he was able to concentrate on reading, music, and everything else.

Sunday school and church the next morning went without incident. His pink burn was practically gone, and he must have looked less uncomfortable since several parishioners gently asked about his experience two Fridays ago. A few ladies even hugged him about it and said they were praying for him. Then he learned Kenley's article had already appeared in that morning's *Gazette*. *Good Lord*, he thought, *she must have worked on it the rest of the day after lunch*. Eager to read it, he took it as a good sign that no one in the family pew mentioned it, either in church or at the family home during Sunday dinner.

Back at his own house, Elton immediately looked up the article on his computer. It was not only the top story on the front page, but the longest he had ever read in the local paper. While initially unnerved at its length, he found the picture of him smiling with Longstreet comforting. Reading the article confirmed it was completely accurate and presented his entire experience chronologically, without exaggeration or understatement. It was well written, totally sympathetic, and never misquoted him. It neither portrayed him as anyone to be pitied nor someone seeking attention. It also addressed each of his theories as to what he may have seen.

Completely impressed, he called the *Gazette* to thank Kenley. She happened to be there and was elated with his unqualified endorsement of the story. It had been the longest of her career, and she had in fact worked on it all afternoon and evening. He felt he had finally unburdened himself of an important task that needed to be done and was relieved it had turned out so well. How dramatically less anxious he was to return to school tomorrow compared with last Sunday, he thought.

CHAPTER 9

Unlike last week, no classes this Monday began with students asking Mr. Peabody about any strange encounters. Outside of class, several teachers and students told him they read Sunday's article and had had no idea just how remarkable and intense an experience he went through. Everyone who spoke to him was supportive, even a few who had not been particularly friendly to him before. Miss Nast and Mr. Sneed still ignored him in the hall as usual, but he tried to be grateful they did not treat him any worse.

The rest of the week went well too. He was satisfied with the lectures, class discussions, test grading, and Thursday's Presbyterian Club meeting. There were even a couple of students he did not know visiting the club for the first time. Especially since they were tongue-tied at why they came, Elton wondered if they just wanted a chance to possibly hear the local UFO man talk about his experience. But the new boy and girl were polite, and Mr. Peabody was delighted the members welcomed them so warmly, as they always did with every visitor.

Elton could concentrate better and was sleeping more too. While still plagued by some unfocused anxiety about the incident and troubled by the questions it raised, he recognized his life appeared to be returning to routine status. Yes, his parents had called more than usual since the event, but he was touched. Melody had also left a phone message and e-mailed to check on her brother. He felt good he had not fallen apart or sought out his old shrink again. He liked her and was so grateful for all her help all those years before, but just the thought of seeing her again unleashed a tide of painful memories. He wanted to believe he was much stronger and in a far more secure chapter of his life than he had been in graduate school. *Just think how much more confident I might be if I navigate this on my own,* he reasoned. Besides, his family and friends had rallied around him. *It will be okay,* he kept repeating.

The one development during his second week since the incident that worried him was the message left on his answer machine by the reporter from the *National Exposure*, the nation's long-time leading tabloid whose subject matter ranged from exposing the sexcapades of politicians and celebrities to revealing how aliens kidnapped folks to perform sex change operations on them aboard their spacecraft. Elton did not dare return the call and hoped nothing would come of it. Nor did he tell anyone since he wanted to reduce his family and friends' worry as much as he could.

But the third Monday since the incident would not be forgotten. School went fine, but his trip to the grocery store on the way home would be surreal. Standing in the checkout line, he could not help but notice the new issue of *The National Exposure*. Normally he smiled at the ridiculously lurid headlines and cartoonish graphics, but not today. There was his picture from last year's high school yearbook under the headline, "HIGH SCHOOL TEACHER KIDNAPPED AND POSSIBLY BRAINWASHED BY UFO." A drawing from a 1950s schlock movie poster portrayed an alien spaceship shining a bright light on his photograph. Elton stood frozen, staring at the magazine. His stomach instantly became a tight knot, and he could feel his heart race. He did not hear the cashier say hello. Instead, he began to feel hot and realized he was perspiring. Reality had returned—on steroids.

When the cashier greeted him a second time, he jumped.

"Oh, I'm sorry, Mr. Peabody! I didn't mean to scare you," Gina Odum tried to reassure him. She had been a student of his a couple of years before.

Elton grabbed a copy of the magazine and hesitated for a second, wondering if he should buy them all to throw away. But he did not want anyone to think he might be craving such publicity. Dazed, he figured he should say something to Gina as to why her former history teacher was buying the most notorious publication in the nation.

"I thought about you, sir. When I saw that, I said, 'Mr. Peabody is sure not going to like this.' I'm so sorry," she told him.

Elton nodded but was having a hard time speaking and did not know what to say anyway. His pale complexion and sad face spoke enough.

"Don't let this bother you, Mr. Peabody. Nobody believes any of that stuff. Everybody will know it's just *The Exposure*. Good to see you, sir," she tried to reassure him.

He paid his bill, nodded at her, and turned to walk away.

"Sir, you forgot your change and groceries," she announced.

He thanked her, gathered his belongings, and headed to the car. He just wanted to be home with General Longstreet. He would read the article and go from there. *Don't panic,* he pleaded.

After taking the general outside, he decided to digest the article on a full stomach. So he loaded up the microwave. But the tension was too great. So he devoured the entire story first—and what a tale it was. He sighed. *The Exposure* claimed he had been abducted by aliens who took him into their spaceship in the woods where experiments were performed on him, including his brain and even "a possible sex change." He moaned. When the aliens finished with him, they spit him out of their craft just before leaving town, but not before messing with his memory so he would not remember anything about them. All the sources were "unnamed," yet they somehow knew crucial aspects to the story that Elton did not. *Maybe these secret sources were little green men,* Elton mused. One unnamed source alleged "Mr. Peabody just hasn't been himself since that night," while another confirmed "He's acted real strange since then." The story itself was not that long due to all the bizarre sci-fi imagery and large print. But also in the story was Sheriff Peabody's quote from Kenley's article announcing the investigation had been reopened. Much worse was the file picture of Bo and the article's assertion that an anonymous "some" were claiming the sheriff was not pursuing the investigation aggressively because of nepotism. Elton groaned again.

What a disaster, he lamented. Sure, everyone with a room temperature IQ knows this is garbage, and how many folks even read such trash? *But everyone will know about it.* The story was likely already traveling throughout the county at light speed. How humiliating, and not just for him, but especially for his brother facing reelection next week. And what about everyone at the school? How awful this publicity must be for Principal Toombs and how secretly thrilled must Assistant Principal Sneed be. What must he brace himself for from students tomorrow? How terrible for the whole town of Cleburne and the county of Johnston, both of which were prominently mentioned in the article. How many locals would now get angry at him for this unwanted and embarrassing attention? Could people seriously think he may have been a source for this nonsense?

Worst of all was what this could mean for his brother's reelection chances. Indeed, while Elton was portrayed as a hapless victim, Bo and his deputies were ridiculed for "their fruitless wild goose chase" pursuing "UFOs" all over the county while Elton was being operated on by surgeons from outer space. Worse, and light years more believable, was the charge the sheriff was refusing to work hard to find out what really happened because of his family tie and concern about how such an effort "could affect his upcoming re-election fight." Elton wondered if ex-deputy Ray Campbell was the source for that dig.

For a long time he sat at the dinner table with his head in his hands as Longstreet sat at his feet patiently. Finally the general whimpered and gently pawed him. Elton sighed and gave him a hug.

"Oh, how I'd love to trade places with you, boy. You have no idea how much better you've got it, fellow. None."

Well, I don't see how it gets much worse than this, he tried to reassure himself. *Unless I get fired for becoming too much of a distraction at school.* Feeling numb, he reheated his dinner and ate it with no musical or television accompaniment. What to do now was his sole concern, especially how to help Bo win reelection. If I lose my reputation and job, it's ultimately my own stupid fault for going after that bloody light. But Bo does not deserve any of this. He's been the best sheriff this county has ever had and is so young that he could go on to tremendous heights in his profession. He's been wonderful to me about this mess and totally professional too. Yet now his name, face, and department are plastered all over the biggest scandal sheet in the country or even the world just two days before the debate with his opponent and eight days before the primary election. *He could very well lose, and it's all my fault,* lamented Elton. *This is so unfair. What would this do to Bo, to Stevie, their girls, and to the whole family? Heck, what about the security of the whole county being tied to that show-off loser, Ray Campbell? I'll have to live with that for the rest of my life.* He sighed. *Dear God, it's all so awful. Why, God? Why?*

His mind was racing in circles and he could not decide what the best course of action was. Should he sue *The Exposure*? Restore his good name and defend Bo, the Sheriff's Department, Cleburne, and Johnston County in the process? But he understood libel law well enough to know he had no case. The story claimed he was "possibly brainwashed" and given a "possible sex change" and, most importantly, he could not prove the paper was guilty of malice or deliberately trying to destroy him personally. Besides, even if he could, a lawsuit would only cause the legitimate press to write about it, making it an even far bigger deal. Imagine all the lawyers' fees, having to testify in legal depositions, perhaps Bo and others having to as well, how many years such a case could go on in the courts, and what such a protracted ordeal could mean for his whole family.

What if he wrote to *The Exposure* with a denial of everything? *Right, as if it would ever be printed,* he figured. *Heck, those jerks might even include it in a follow-up article as "proof" I've been brainwashed. Another bad option,* he concluded.

More immediately, how to prepare for tomorrow's classes and the inevitable gibes and questions about their now infamous joke of a history teacher? *Best to hit them head on with another humor routine to try to ridicule and laugh at the story,* he figured. *I better meet privately with Principal Toombs too and stress how sorry I am about the whole thing and promise how it's not affecting my classes.* For the first time, he feared his job could well be in serious jeopardy. The thought of being fired and having to try to find a teaching gig in another county was too much to bear at the moment. Since this *Exposure* article was in most every grocery in the nation, he might not be able to get another teaching position anywhere. Then what would he do?

Worried about what his family might be going through, imagining how worried his parents must be about him and Bo, and yearning for his parents to help him decide what to do, he drove to the family farm. They were not surprised when he arrived. After greeting him warmly, he asked if they had heard about or read the *Exposure* piece. They confirmed they had and stressed no one would believe such nonsense. Sitting in the den, Elton apologized for having caused the family so much pain and embarrassment with his breakdown years before and now this. He would do whatever they thought would help the family the most.

"Now, Elton, stop," his father ordered, raising his hand for emphasis. "Now you have done nothing wrong here. Not when you went to the hospital or over this article. Your mother and I applaud how hard you worked to recover years back and what a super success you've made of yourself. And as for this ridiculous story, everybody knows that rag prints nothing but trash, and nobody respectable believes it."

"Your father's right, Elton," his mother pronounced. "There's no need for you to let this foolishness upset you so."

"I could lose my job, Momma," Elton stressed. "This is exactly what Frank Sneed needs to try to go after me."

"Honey, that man has made more enemies than anyone in the whole Johnston County school system," she declared. "You know what a fine Christian gentleman Principal Toombs is. You have nothing to worry about with your job."

His father added, "Son, for your own peace of mind, why don't you go talk with Bob tomorrow and tell him how unfortunate you think this story is, assure him you're fine, and see for yourself he's on your side. He knows what a great job you do at that school. Everybody does. Now don't let this get the better of you, Elton. You've been handling this thing real well. Your mother and I were just talking about what a super job you've done and how you haven't let it interfere with your work or anything. You can handle this, son. Just stay strong."

After pausing to not get emotional, Elton promised to talk with Mr. Toombs tomorrow. Then he asked what he should do to help Bo.

"Don't you fret one bit about your brother, Elton," said his mother. "The voters know full well what a first-rate job he's done for this county. And they sure know he's a whole far sight better than Ray Campbell. I wouldn't be a bit surprised if that snake in the grass is responsible for a lot of that *Exposure* story. Bo is going to do just fine in Wednesday's debate and then he's going to win next Tuesday. And he knows none of this is your fault."

"And if you don't believe that, then you ask him," his father added. "Bo knows just how to handle stuff like this…and the people around these parts ain't stupid. They know what's going on."

"Maybe I should write my own account of what really happened and make a point of how wonderful a job Bo and the deputies have done throughout this whole thing," Elton speculated.

After a pause, his mother pleaded, "Elton, you've got your whole life to figure out and write about this episode. What's the rush? Like your father said, you've handled this so well. You're dealing with it far better than a whole heck of a lot of folks would. We're real proud of you, dear. But why dwell on this thing another minute more than absolutely necessary. If you write an article, it's just going to make it an even bigger deal and stress you out all the more. Nobody needs that, Elton, especially you. Don't worry about Bo. Or your father and mother or Melody. Everyone is doing well and admiring how well you're handling things."

Elton thanked them and expressed how grateful he was for all their love, support, and help. Though he still felt awful, he was better than when he arrived. The conversation turned to far lighter family and farm matters, and then church affairs came up. His mother gently urged him to consider seeking out the counsel of the Rev. Presseau. She reminded him how helpful their pastor had been to all of them years before and how well he often spoke of Elton. Her son said he was still thinking about it and would not hesitate if matters got much worse. Then he wondered how much worse they could get.

He silently resolved to talk with Bo as soon as he could to say how sorry he was and ask how best to help with the election. Perhaps he could help him prepare for the debate.

Back home that evening, he played an extra-long time with the general, not being able to concentrate on much else. He tried hard to just zero in on the here and now of throwing a tennis ball and relishing the uninhibited joy his dog displayed. *I should learn from him,* he thought.

As much as he wanted to talk with Bo that night, he could not bring himself to pick up the phone or drive over to his brother's home. While confident his brother would be completely understanding, Elton felt too fatigued and did not want to deal with the matter just yet. He resolved to go see him tomorrow, preferably at his office, so they could have more privacy.

School the next day was difficult but not nearly as bad as Elton had dreaded. Yes, three of his classes began with some students laughing and asking about the *Exposure* story. He had done his best to laugh and try to make fun of it. But he did not come across as wittily as he had that Monday right after the story broke, or at least the students did not laugh as much. He also cut off the UFO questions much quicker this time and was extra serious and fast-paced in his lectures. In the two classes that did not start with students asking about the latest story, he could sense some added tension and definitely noted several smiles in class that did not appear connected to any opening announcements he made. So he launched a preemptive strike by bringing up the story to lampoon it before quickly turning to the day's lecture.

During his lunch hour he went straight to Principal Toombs's office. While waiting for him to finish with someone else, Elton tried to review exactly what he would say. Before he got far, the door flew open and Assistant Principal Sneed walked out, always in a hurry. *Great,* Elton thought, *I wonder what that was about.* While they looked at each other briefly, neither spoke.

"Come on in, Elton!" boomed Principal Toombs. *Well, that sounded good,* he thought. The men shook hands and sat down.

Though he usually started off with small talk, this time Elton went straight to why he was there.

"Principal Toombs, I am so very sorry about this outrageous *National Exposure* article and all the unwanted attention it's caused. I had nothing to do with it and it's, of course, totally absurd. This job means so much to me, sir. It's the center of my life, and I want you to know I would never do or say anything to ever detract from the education of our students. None of this whole stupid UFO nightmare has impacted my lectures or any other responsibilities here. I'm so sorry, and I will do or say whatever you want me to about all this, whatever you think will help the school the most."

"Elton, I appreciate all that very much. I really do, and you have nothing to worry about. I know—everyone knows—this is just an unfortunate situation that this national scandal rag has taken advantage of. I know you're doing your normal fine job of teaching. There's not been one report of any of this affecting you. And the students get it. They know this is a totally bogus story. In fact, especially after that big spread in Sunday's *Gazette* when the full, actual story came out, a lot of folks have remarked what an amazing thing you went through, how brave you were, and just how well you've handled it."

"Thank you, sir, I really appreciate that."

"So don't you worry about this. I appreciate you're coming here today on your own volition to express your concern about the school. I know how much you love your students and care about Johnston High. We all do. Now it's almost class time. So you better get ready. But thank you for stopping by, Elton."

"Principal Toombs, thank you. More than I could ever express."

The rest of the day went much better. He thanked God for good men like his principal and envied his boss's strength, quiet confidence, and decency. He also resolved to try to have more sympathy for students and anyone else going through tough times and do all he could to help.

When he got home and heard a prank call message on his answer machine related to the *Exposure* story, he erased it as soon as he realized he did not know the caller. Though angered, he also chuckled a bit and was surprised it did not bother him a lot more.

As always, General Longstreet helped. It was such a splendid smiler to have somebody in his life who was always happy and even thrilled to see him. They played fetch the tennis ball for a long time after dinner, perhaps because Elton was dreading the call he promised himself to make to his brother. He felt sure Bo would not be angry at him, but abhorred diving back into that whole swamp again. When he realized playing with his dog could no longer hide the task from view, he brought the general back inside.

He did not call his brother's home since he did not want to deal with Bo's wife Stevie if it could be avoided, at least not now. He and his sister-in-law had always gotten along and never argued, but he knew she was very protective of her husband and had seen her get strident when angry. He was certain the *Exposure* article would have her livid. No, she would know he had not contributed to the story in any way. But he could see her contending he was still partly responsible since he had foolishly pursued that weird light in the woods—and at night and all by himself.

Though she was already Bo's college sweetheart at the time, Elton and Stevie had never mentioned his hospitalization to each other. She was a strong lady who, though sweet and principled, was not shy expressing her views. He imagined her seeing him as much weaker than her husband and wondered if she berated Bo for being too protective of his older brother, particularly during this UFO mess.

So he called the Sheriff's Department. Just hearing Casandra's cheerful voice answer the phone was always an emotional lift. She had been a fun student to have in class four years before for taking a wry view of history and none of its actors too seriously. He particularly appreciated her witty remarks about its most serious, constipated characters. It was always rewarding to be prompted into seeing people from a different perspective. She also asked pointed, off-beat questions he had not expected, forcing him to reexamine subjects from other angles.

He grew even fonder of her for doing so much to help Bo get elected while still a high school senior. While he knew how smart and successful a student she was, he was mightily impressed at all the organizational and leadership skills she displayed during the campaign. She even put together a "Students for Peabody" team that put up more campaign posters around the county than anyone else.

Elton was delighted when the new sheriff hired her as his secretary. Still just eighteen when she began the job, she impressed everyone with her ability to seamlessly meld professionalism with girlish charm. She was extremely efficient, totally loyal to her boss, and willing to work long hours because she loved the job and the excitement of being "in the center of where it all goes down in Johnston County," as she laughingly put it. Best of all, her sharp sense of humor had only gotten more seasoned, and she brought such a positive energy to the whole Sheriff's Department that everyone treasured.

"Johnston County Sheriff's Department. How can we help?"

"Hey, Miss Casandra. How are you, dear?"

"Mr. Peabody! I'm fine. How are you doing on this terrific Tuesday?"

"Ah…okay. Just trying to reach Bo if I could, please."

"He's taken Stevie and the girls out for dinner, but then he's coming back to the office to work late. He often takes the family out on the town on days he's got to pull a late-nighter. That usually settles things down on the home front." She giggled. "Want me to leave him a note you called?"

"Please. Thanks, Casandra, and thank you for all you do for Bo and the whole department and really for this entire county. We're all blessed you're there doing such a superb job."

"Well, thank you, Mr. Peabody. That's mighty sweet of you. I really appreciate that. In fact, coming from my favorite teacher, that means more than you'll ever know. I wish you taught at Stonewall Jackson College. But thank you. I love my job and it's a real friendly place to work, and your brother's really a big softie. I'll leave him your message."

CHAPTER 10

Sheriff Peabody took Stevie and their two young daughters, Sarah and Esther, to the children's favorite local eatery, Mr. Allen's Grill. It was one of the most popular restaurants in Cleburne and the most prominent black eatery. The girls adored its signature French fries, which were far better than the ones at fast food chains. They also loved the waitresses for being the friendliest in town. The staff would hug the girls, exclaim how pretty they were, and even take them by the hand to the kitchen when the children wanted to see how their favorite fries were made.

Outside of the Bethel African Methodist Episcopal Church and Ebenezer Baptist Church, Mr. Allen's Grill had for decades been the most important public meeting place for the local black community. But the white community patronized the place as well. Mr. Zechariah Allen had long been a local institution. Large, loud, and friendly, he liked to greet diners when they arrived and walk from table to table chatting with everyone. His *joie de vivre* made all feel welcome. And the Peabody daughters would squeal laughing at the older gentleman's remarkable imitation of their father. Sheriff and Mrs. Peabody enjoyed it too.

Sheriff Peabody was particularly grateful to Mr. Allen for putting his campaign poster in the restaurant's front window four years before and this year as well. In fact, Bo's election victory party had been held at the restaurant, and Mr. Allen told him he would be hurt something terrible if this year's election night get-together was not held there again.

Bo treasured his friendship with the older gentleman. He had known him his whole thirty-three years, ever since his parents first brought him to the restaurant as a baby. Growing up, Bo, Elton, and Melody loved how Mr. Allen went out of his way to talk with them and actually listen to what they had to say. No other businessman had ever made such time for them growing up. Best of all, he never failed to crack them up with his kidding and over-the-top impressions of folks, especially their father, a former classmate and life-long friend. When little, Bo and his siblings would explode laughing as Mr. Allen would walk and talk like their old man while the whole family sat right there. Both Momma and Daddy laughed as well.

In high school, Mr. Allen gave Bo his first part-time job. His son, Isaiah, was a teammate of Bo on the football team who vouched for what a solid student and reliable team player the young Peabody was. So Bo became the first white worker at the restaurant. Though he got a few surprised looks from black and white patrons when he began his stint as a busboy, the staff embraced him since they had known him his whole life, liked his family, and cheered him on the football field at all the Johnston County High home games each fall. After working there a while, Bo asked Mr. Allen what made him the first white employee.

"Boy, you're the first one that ever applied." He laughed.

After Bo graduated from high school and went on to other jobs, he remained friends with Isaiah and the entire Allen family. When he ran for sheriff the first time, the Allens and everyone at the restaurant were big supporters. Bo knew that, without their backing and, through their help, the votes of most of the black neighborhoods, he would not have won. In fact, he lost the white vote. So he considered it critical to maintain his strength on the black side of the railroad tracks. He had hired a record number of black deputies and increased patrols in black neighborhoods, both by car and foot. In every neighborhood, black and white, he had his deputies, black and white, make a point of reaching out to folks, getting on a first-name basis with the neighbors, and playing ball in the street with their children. These efforts had borne positive fruit in persuading many locals to report crimes who had never done so before.

Like four years before, Bo spoke at the county's two largest black churches during his reelection campaign. This time he summarized what he saw as the Sheriff's Department's significant achievements over the last four years. He had been warmly received at both houses of worship and was confident the black vote would again break his way. But the whole UFO drama was a wild card on both sides of the tracks.

Fortunately for the Peabody campaign, ex-deputy and campaign rival Ray Campbell did not have remotely the same reputation with most black Johnston Countians. Many thought he had never shown them the same friendly face he was liked for on the other side of the county. Indeed, when visiting the county seat of Cleburne, they had seen how gregarious and jovial he was with white residents. Yet he appeared stiff and removed with them. And no one could recall his ever patrolling much in their neighborhoods unless he was answering a 911 call. Bo hoped they remembered all that next Tuesday in the voting booth.

When Sarah and Esther's favorite waitress, Priscilla Holmes, took them by hand to the kitchen to see how their favorite blueberry pies got prepared, Stevie turned to her husband.

"All right, Bo. What's the fallout from this *Exposure* story?"

Her husband's smile turned into a frown as he sighed and looked up at the ceiling. He and his wife had each been so busy since the tabloid hit the groceries the day before that they had yet to discuss it. The election was just a week out, and both were concerned about what this latest story could mean for them. Just when the local *Gazette* had stopped its almost daily articles on "the local lights," *The Exposure* had swooped down like a hungry hawk to bring more worry.

"Honey bunny, I just don't know. On the plus side, the whole piece is so plainly stupid that I just hate to think we've got many folks here who would believe any of it. I know a lot of locals will likely buy a copy because the cover story is local and Elton's picture's on the front-page. But I believe a whole lot of them will feel right embarrassed they bought the thing once they read the story."

"Well, what about its charge you're dragging your feet on the investigation and covering for your brother?"

Bo again sighed.

"And your picture being in it too?"

"I know. I know," he said softly. "But I expect this UFO thing is starting to get old around here. I got a feeling not nearly as many folks who were all hot for some highfalutin' investigation two weeks ago are still hankering for such."

"What about the charge you're covering something for Elton?"

Squinting his eyes and expanding his nostrils, Bo's voice became more adamant.

"It's not true. Not at all. There's nothing to hide. Elton told us everything that night, and Miss Cassie typed up the whole report. And then he relayed the whole thing again for everybody in the *Gazette.* And I got to give that new reporter, Miss Kitchens, credit 'cause she laid it all out exactly as Elton told it to me and Otis.

"And we *have* continued to investigate whatever may have happened that night. I personally called all the nearest military bases to ask about any possible night flights, and the boys and I have talked with dozens of witnesses, taking good notes and getting Cassie to type up every single one of them. And they're all on file for everyone to see too."

"I know, Shug. You've handled this extremely well—a dang sight better than I would have. But you've got to get the word out about all this to the public. I don't know how else you can rest easy that this thing won't trip you up next Tuesday.

"How's Elton? I know you and your folks keep saying he's handling this a whole lot better than y'all thought he might, but that was before *The Exposure* story yesterday."

"I can't say, babe. If he doesn't call tonight, I'll call or stop by his place. I'm real worried about him."

Rubbing his shoulder and feeling how tense his muscles were, she began massaging them with both hands.

"Bo. I know you love your brother, and I do too. He's a fine man. And I know you're protective of him, especially since he went to the hospital way back when. But, honey, he's a thirty-five-year-old man now. He's a big boy. And he's your *older* brother. I know you want to protect him, but there's only so much you can do to shield him from all the mean people out there who are going to inevitably try to take advantage of this 'UFO' mess. That's just comes with the territory.

"And he was the one who chose to go out by himself at night chasing that light in the woods. I would have *never* expected him of all people to do such a thing. I'm sorry he had this awful experience, but it's done and there's only so much you can do to try to shield him from the inevitable fallout. And he was the one who gave that *Gazette* reporter the interview. Heck, maybe that's what drew *The Exposure* to cover this. I don't know."

"*The Exposure* story had to already be in the works. But I know, Stevie. I can't disagree with what all you've said. Still, I know how fragile he can be. Yes, he's handled this whole thing real well so far, way better than I feared he would. But I just keep thinking back to when he had that nervous breakdown that put him in the hospital. We almost lost him, Stevie. Momma told me his doctor told her and Daddy he was suicidal. Heck, they even found a note. That was a real rough time for the whole family. It took a whole lot out of Momma and Daddy, and I don't want anything like that to happen again. It's just such a shame this all had to happen and right before the election too."

Leaning her head on his shoulder, his wife put her arms around him and pulled him tight.

"You're a good man, Beauregard Peabody, and Mrs. Peabody is right proud of you. And you are going to win this election."

Breaking into a grin for the first time in a while, Bo thanked her just before Priscilla returned with the girls, each of whom was beaming with a piece of blueberry pie on the house. Bo soon dropped off his family at the house before returning to the office to finish up his paperwork and address some campaign chores Cassie had been after him about.

As he walked by her desk just outside his glassed-in office, she gave him Elton's message. Stopping midstride, he paused and asked her to call him back to see if he could please just stop by the office tonight.

"Tell him I've got a slew of paperwork and campaign stuff to do. So it'll be a late-nighter and he can come anytime."

Cassie did so and then hijacked her boss to approve several campaign ideas and speaking engagements she wanted him to commit to before the election. She knew how devoted her boss was to his big brother and figured they might have a long talk that evening. So she wanted the sheriff's full attention before he got distracted.

Elton arrived about eight. Cassie was walking out of her boss's office, having just gotten some more papers signed before filing them. Her grin at greeting her old history teacher always gave him a smile. She gave him a big hug, and Elton thought she pulled him a tad tighter and held him just a little longer than she had before.

"Your brother's waiting on you. Go on in."

He did and she closed the glass door behind him.

Bo stood up with a smile and extended his hand.

"Hey, buddy. Come on in. Have a seat. What's up?

Elton sat down, sighed, and looked at his brother smiling at him. He started to speak and then stopped.

"I'm awful blessed to have a brother who's always so kind and cheerful with me despite my continuing to cause him trouble," Elton announced softly.

"You haven't caused me trouble. I'm blessed to have such a fine role model of an older brother," Bo replied.

"Thanks. But you're too kind. Bo, I feel just terrible about this *Exposure* story. Just when Kenley and *The Gazette* had stopped covering the 'UFOs' and I thought the story was starting to go away, here comes this *Exposure* nonsense, right on time. And I had nothing to do with it."

"Of course not. I know that. Everybody does."

Elton leaned over the desk, both elbows on it and his hands gesturing.

"I thought by telling Miss Kenley the whole story so everybody in these parts would know what really happened, that that would help end it. So much for my strategy. Heck, maybe the *Exposure* 'reporter' read my interview on the Internet which gave him the idea to write about this."

"It had to have already been in the pipeline, Elton."

"But for your picture to be in that bloody rag, and the stupid charge you're not investigating what happened when several *Gazette* articles have reported about all the witnesses y'all've already interviewed and how you've even gotten in touch with military bases and on and on. And all this right before your debate tomorrow night—which you should probably be preparing for but instead you're having to hold the hand of your *big* brother, again—and your election is next week. If you lose, it'll be because of me. It's my fault, Bo. If I hadn't been so stupid as to go out in the woods that night, by myself, after that crazy light and never turn around. Oh, no. Mr. UFO couldn't botch his big chance for his very own *close encounter*. More like Mr. F. Dufus Stupet.

"My selfishness has hurt you, our family, your family, and the whole Sheriff's Department. It's distracted the whole county and now we've all been embarrassed before the whole country. And the end result of all this may well be a Sheriff Ray Campbell. My selfish stupidity may cost my own brother his job—Stevie's husband and y'all's little girls' daddy."

With that, Elton broke down and began sobbing with his head in his hands.

"I'm so sorry, Bo. I'm so sorry. Can you ever forgive me? I'm sorry."

Bo swallowed and leaned forward.

"Elton, listen to me. Now listen to me. You have done nothing wrong. Nothing. What you did that night was what a whole lot of us would have done. I would have. Especially any UFO buff like yourself. If you hadn't, you'd be kicking yourself now and regretting it for the rest of your life."

"Not like I'm regretting all this," Elton cried.

"This will pass, buddy. And one day, and I believe soon, we'll all be able to laugh about it. You've got quite a story to tell for the rest of your life, and it's all true too and documented…though I'm not including that *Exposure* piece." He smiled.

Elton managed a bitter chuckle.

"And you haven't hurt anyone, Elton. Everyone's handling this well. Momma, Daddy, Melody, me, Stevie, and the girls, the department—heck, most of the boys have been thrilled to investigate this thing—and the whole county's loved reading and speculating all about its very own *UFOs*. I'm tempted to ask *The Gazette* how many more papers they've sold since covering this story. In fact, you and I ought to get a free lifetime subscription. You saw all those big front-page articles Miss Kenley wrote on it. Heck, boy, you helped make her career. Shoot, that cute gal ought to ask you out and treat you to dinner."

"She has a boyfriend."

"All right. Whatever. We live in a fallen world. But you've handled all this so well, Elton. Momma and Daddy and Melody and I can't get over how well…we're just super impressed."

"Yeah, look at me," Elton replied, blowing his nose.

"Come on, man. You know what I mean. You're a far sight stronger now than you've ever been." After a long pause, "And I bet what put you in the hospital twelve years ago wasn't as stressful as what you've endured of late."

Elton had stopped crying and stared at the desk, listening. He felt so drained and wondered when his life would ever get back to anything qualifying as normal.

"And don't you worry about me and my career, Elton. I appreciate that. I really do. But I don't want you to give that another thought. I'm telling you I'm going to win. This department has done a good job these last four years. In fact, I think it's doing better than ever. And I believe the data prove it too. Drugs and gangs aren't nearly as bad. We've got far better relations with the community than before—and on *both* sides of the tracks. And we've even logged a lot of interviews about these lights. But neither are we obsessing about it or neglecting any of our responsibility keeping folks safe. So nobody can get away with saying we've dropped the ball on that, either.

"And frankly, Elton, if the voters of Johnston County are so dumb as to think we've either done too much on this UFO thing or not enough, or that I've somehow covered up for you, then I don't want this job. But that's not what people tell me. I get almost nothing but positive vibes from everyone I talk to about the election. And believe me, brother, there are folks who would absolutely tell me if things looked bad. Heck, with our record over the last four years, I'm a whole lot better known now than I was four years ago. And a lot of folks just vote for the incumbent anyway.

"And we're doing real well in the black community. I got a tremendous reception at every black church I've spoke at this year, even warmer than the last time I ran. And they know I've spoken to them and visited them several times since the last election too. And black folks know better than anyone how much Ray Campbell thinks about them. Plus a lot of black and white folks know the real reason he was fired too. It may not have made *The Gazette*, but I guarantee you the Johnston County gossip express sure spread the news."

Elton had listened closely and had to admit his brother was making a lot of sense. He still felt awful, but it was a comfort that, intellectually at least, things did not appear nearly as bleak as they felt.

"It will be okay, buddy. We're going to win this debate tomorrow night. We're going to win that election next Tuesday. And, even if we don't, we're going to all go on with our lives and this thing is just going to be an ever-smaller blip in our rearview mirror."

Elton took a deep breath, swallowed, and nodded. "I hope you're right. You make a lot of sense. I sure hope so."

"You know I'm right. Like Daddy says, we need to always think positively. There's no use thinking negatively. Life's tough enough as it is. Negative thinking only makes it worse. Nothing gets done without hope. And remember what Momma and Daddy have always told us about the importance of faith. It's helped us all get through every one of our struggles. Momma and Daddy are real proud of you, Elton. You've always been a good son to them and you came back from that hospital and became a wonderful history teacher. Nobody would ever think you were anything else. You earned that, buddy. And I'm real proud to call you my brother."

With that, Elton let out a quiet sob, hiding his tears again with his hand. Not expecting that and not knowing what else to say, Bo reached across the desk and took his brother's hand. They had not held hands since they were small children. After a while Elton squeezed his brother's hand, blew his nose, and stood up to thank him and say goodbye. Bo walked around the desk and they embraced. Elton bit his tongue hard to keep from breaking down again. They each smiled at the other and then Elton got out his handkerchief to wipe away his tears before facing the world again. He did not want his former student to see he had been crying.

His former student had been diligently working at her desk throughout the meeting. Casandra cared deeply for both men and knew what their talk was about. Though intensely interested, she tried her best not to look through the window at them. But when she had to get up to make some copies, she could not help seeing Elton bent over with his head in his hands appearing to sob. The sight startled her. She had never seen one of her teachers cry, and seeing a grown man weep had always been a little frightening. She so wanted to help Mr. Peabody but did not know how. She also felt for her boss. How terribly tough this must all be for him as well. Just because he did not shed tears did not mean he was not in a heap of hurt too, she figured.

Later, and not intending to, she happened to look up from her desk just as the sheriff reached across his desk to take his brother's hand. Casandra swallowed. When she saw the brothers embrace, she felt her own tears and quickly went to the ladies' room.

On the drive home, Elton did not listen to the radio as he usually did when driving. Instead, he tried to remember all Bo had said and just relish the best sense of well-being he had felt in some time. Keep telling myself it will be okay, he implored. Everything will work out. It always does. I've been through so much worse and I *am* stronger than before. And the worst is over.

11

CHAPTER

Wednesday at school went well for Mr. Peabody. He had slept better the night before and was pleased with most of his lectures. Though disappointed with the one where he had gotten distracted thinking about recent events, he was surprised at how little it bothered him afterward. And, though nervous about the big debate that evening, he was also optimistic Bo would do well.

But when he stopped at a drugstore on the way home to get some milk, he could not miss the front page of the local *Gazette* near the check-out counter. The sub-heading to the lead story, "SHERIFF'S DEBATE TONIGHT," read: "CAMPBELL ACCUSES DEPARTMENT OF 'BOTCHING' UFO INVESTIGATION." Reality had returned and right on time, Elton thought bitterly.

Devouring the article as soon as he got home, Elton got angry. Though the last three weeks had been a time of extreme emotion for him, he had experienced mostly feelings of fear, shock, dread, confusion, frustration, and sadness. But now he became the angriest he had been in some time. Sheriff's candidate and ex-deputy Ray Campbell charged his opponent with "grossly wasting the depart-ment's limited resources on a wild UFO goose chase." Yet he also accused his former employer with limiting the investigation "to try to save his own brother and family from further embarrassment."

What an evil, unmitigated jerk, Elton fumed. If Bo had had his dru-thers and there was no investigation, Campbell would have screamed about the lack of one. Now that there is one, somehow it's already been "botched" because the Johnston County Sheriff's Department has yet to un-riddle the mystery of UFOs—like everyone else.

The phone rang. In the last three weeks, Elton had screened his calls. The phone number flashing on his phone was that of *The Gazette*. Did they want a comment about the article? You bet they would sure get one, and maybe they could print at least some of it after deleting all the choicest words.

"Hello," he almost barked into the receiver. General Longstreet looked up at him.

"Hey, Elton! It's Kenley. How are you?"

"Oh. Hi." For some reason, he had not expected she would be on the line, even though she had written the article he just read.

"I was wondering if you'd read today's *Gazette* article about tonight's debate that I wrote."

"Actually, I just read it."

"I almost called you last night about it, Elton, to give you a heads-up because I felt badly about quoting Mr. Campbell and all the stuff he said. But then I didn't want to take a chance on worry-ing you and maybe interfering with your sleep. I'm sorry about the article including all those nasty swipes he took. Unfortunately, since I'm covering the campaign, I have to report what the candidates say, even if it's awful."

"I understand completely, Kenley. You have nothing for which to apologize. I'm angry at Ray, not you."

"I did quote your brother rebutting his stupid charges."

"I know and I appreciate that and I'm sure he does too. Thanks."

"Are you doing okay? I mean, I'm sure you saw that terrible *Exposure* piece. I've been thinking about you and hoping you didn't let it upset you. I wanted to call you about it but thought maybe you might not want to talk about it. Are you all right?"

"Yes. It's been upsetting, but I'm getting through it. School's been good and I had a great talk about it with Bo last night. We'll both be glad when this election's over."

"I'm sure. Are you going to the debate tonight?"

"Oh, yes. I expect the entire family will be there. We'll all sit together."

"Cool. I'll see you there. I'd love to meet your folks. And, Elton, I think you're handling all this exposure remarkably well. A lot of folks would crack under this kind of spotlight. I don't know what I would do."

"Thanks very much, Kenley. I appreciate that. Your interview and article helped a lot. Thank you."

"Okeydoke. See you at the debate!"

Why do the all the gals who seem so perfect always have a boyfriend, Elton thought. *Without exception. I guess it's because they're practically perfect, like Mary Poppins. Reality.*

The auditorium in the courthouse that evening was full, with many folks standing along the walls and in the back. There were even people sitting on the floor down front. Elton arrived just before the debate began at seven and would not have gotten a seat if his mother had not saved him one with the family near the front. His sister, Melody, had driven all the way from her home to support her brother as well. Stevie sat next to her father-in-law, Joshua Peabody, but Sarah and Esther were home with a sitter since their parents did not want them to hear Daddy verbally attacked in public. Seeing so many supporters of Bo's buoyed the family's spirits. No one brought up that morning's *Gazette* article or Ray Campbell's latest charges against the Sheriff's Department.

Elton was delighted to be seated between his mother and Casandra who each gave him a hug. Casandra was the closest thing to a campaign manager Bo had. She was the one who made him repeatedly practice answering tough potential debate questions in the days leading up to the big night. She believed Bo could put the election away that evening if he clearly presented what an excellent record his department had put together these last four years. Her biggest concern was how her boss would respond if Ray went nasty. Everyone knew how angry the ex-deputy was toward the man who fired him. And then there was the whole recent UFO matter. Lord only knows how that could impact tonight, she wondered.

There were only two candidates debating, and each would make a brief opening statement to start the event. WCNE Radio's Mason T. Phillips and Tammy Jean Robards were the debate moderators who would then rotate asking questions for the first forty-five minutes. Then members of the audience could line up at the public microphone to ask questions during the last forty-five minutes. The affair was broadcast live on WCNE and the local TV access channel, and Kenley was covering it for *The Gazette*.

The proceedings began with all standing to recite the Pledge of Allegiance to the American flag. Then the First United Methodist Church preacher, the Rev. Nathanael Simpson, had a prayer. The three largest churches in the county by far were First Baptist, First Presbyterian, and First Methodist. Since Ray Campbell attended the first and Bo Peabody the second, both candidates agreed the Rev. Simpson could give the prayer.

The Peabodys were nervous but cautiously confident. Stevie, in particular, was a knot of nerves. She was infuriated by Ray's accusations in the morning paper and urged her man to rebut each one before going after Ray's extensive womanizing, and without mercy. Bo had patiently heard her out but remained convinced Cassie's advice of remaining firmly on the high road and not losing his temper was the wiser course.

Elton was tense but relieved the matter was out of his hands. He had faith in his brother's proven capacity to keep calm in the midst of terrific stress when everyone else was excited. As much as part of him agreed with his sister-in-law, he suspected Ray may have waited so late to make his insulting charges to try to get the sheriff to lose his temper in the debate.

Mr. and Mrs. Peabody were very proud of all their children and were pleased the whole family had turned out to support one of their own at such an important event. They did not presume to give their second son advice about the debate or the campaign unless he asked, and he had not. Just as Bo gave them a sanitized version of his work life, he was careful to try to protect them from learning about the sleazier aspects of political campaigns, such as his suspicion that

Campbell supporters had been taking down some Peabody signs and even replacing them with Campbell posters.

Sheriff Peabody looked out at the audience and tried to focus on all those he knew were supporting him. He was honored all his family but his young children were there, as well as so many friends. He had the notecards Miss Cassie had made to remind him of all the major points and statistics he wanted to share, and he had added several of his own notes. There were a few butterflies in his stomach, but he knew his secretary had grilled him well in their practice debates. He thought back to when he had debated other opponents four years before and how far more nervous he was then. Now he had an impressive record to share and was much more confident. And as angry as he was at Ray's latest charges, he would not let them get his goat. He was going to be as statesmanlike as possible and just lay out the facts, calmly defend himself when attacked, and never in anger. *Answer each question and stick to my game plan,* he repeated.

A coin toss determined former deputy Campbell would make the first opening statement. He had been waiting years for this moment, ever since being fired by the man standing at the opposite podium just a few feet to his right. After twenty-one years of likely being the most popular deputy on the force, Ray's termination had been the most shocking, humiliating event of his life. He had loved being a deputy, it had been his only job after high school, and he had never prepared for any other profession. The loss of his beloved career in law enforcement had rocked his whole world for the worse. He was so bored being a car salesman, and his marriage had suffered when his wife finally asked if allegations of affairs with other women at work caused his dismissal. He had denied them all as vicious lies spread by a new sheriff who, behind his gentlemanly bark, was an ambitious, career-obsessed back-stabber who saw her far more popular and charismatic husband as a threat to his long-term tenure as sheriff. With the help of his supporters, Ray had convinced himself he was much more qualified to be sheriff. In fact, he had twice as much experience in the department. And now he was determined to hit a home run.

After clearing his throat, Ray began. "Ladies and gentlemen, I'm running for sheriff because I want to restore the quality of law enforcement this county enjoyed for decades under the previous sheriff. Unfortunately, under the present sheriff, things have gotten worse—a whole lot worse. And if that isn't the case, then how do you explain the tremendous support my campaign has gotten? Before Mr. Peabody took over as sheriff, we had an experienced, highly capable Sheriff's Department. But the present sheriff got rid of a lot of that experience for no reason other than he feels threatened by strong colleagues. Anybody who's popular with the public is seen as too big of a potential threat, someone he thinks might one day want his job. And everything must be his way or the highway. He won't take any criticism or suggestions from his employees. So he's brought in too many young, rookie deputies with no experience who won't challenge him. This has reduced the quality of local law enforcement, and all of Johnston County has suffered.

"I've got twenty-one years' law enforcement experience, and all right here in this department. That's twice as much as my opponent. Sheriff Stevens and I worked closely together to bring this county the kind of top-quality law enforcement that y'all saw fit to reelect for decades. I know this county like the back of my hand, and you can bet your bottom dollar, with a Sheriff Campbell-run department, we will bring back the first-rate policing we enjoyed for so long under the previous sheriff. Thank you."

There was a lot of applause, which sent a shiver through many Peabody supporters, especially his family and Casandra. Since there had been no polling, no one knew how much of a threat Campbell really posed to Sheriff Peabody.

The sheriff then made his opening statement. "Fellow Johnston Countians, it has been the greatest honor of my life to serve y'all as sheriff these last four years. I am so humbled you gave me your trust four years ago, and I believe I have honored that trust and ask you to please let me serve you for the next four years.

"During my tenure as sheriff, the department has acquired more deputies than ever before—outstanding young men—and we have instituted a record amount of modern community policing. We have increased the number of foot patrols in neighborhoods, especially those afflicted by the most crime, so our deputies can get to know folks on a friendly, first-name basis. They'll stop and play ball with the children. They run errands for elderly shut-ins. And the department now sponsors and coaches Little League and intermural sports teams from low-income neighborhoods, providing uniforms and equipment for underprivileged children who otherwise couldn't afford to play. Most of these boys don't have a father at home. And so our deputies provide desperately needed strong, positive adult male role models for them.

"We've also worked closer with the local schools than ever before—visiting them a whole lot more, giving presentations on the dangers of drugs and gangs, and getting to know many students on a first-name basis. We've launched a Scared Straight program with both the middle and high schools to help mentor at-risk youth.

"I'm also pleased every single one of our deputies is a church-going member of a local congregation. Our deputies are all fine Christian gentlemen with whom I am so proud to serve.

"And the results of all these efforts to recruit good deputies and reach out to become a lot more involved in the neighborhoods have been better relations between the Sheriff's Department and the entire community and significant reductions in local drug and gang activities.

"If you elect me for another term as your sheriff, I promise this department will continue to build upon all these efforts to bring the best law enforcement we can. Thank you."

At this point there was an enormous round of applause that easily dwarfed what Campbell had gotten. The Peabody supporters were confident their man had hit a home run in his first at bat. Casandra was thrilled at how well her boss had delivered the opening statement she helped write and made him repeatedly rehearse. Elton was elated Bo had gotten off to such a swell start and received such an enthusiastic reception.

Ray Campbell looked uncomfortable and took a drink of water. He had never considered his rival capable of delivering such an eloquent statement, yet it was obvious the sheriff was well prepared and his quiet, even-keeled delivery was appealing to the audience. Indeed, it was the explosively positive response which Peabody garnered that really rattled him. He reminded himself this was their only debate and the election was just six days away. It looked like he might have an uphill battle and he had less than ninety minutes to score a knockout. He decided to go negative to hopefully throw Mr. Calm and Cool off his game.

The questions from Mr. Phillips and Mrs. Robards were the standard stuff of such debates, asking each candidate to specify what kinds of policies he would pursue to combat various types of crime. Each candidate came across as reasonably answering every question, though Sheriff Peabody had a lot more data and specific examples to support his claims. As he watched the clock on the wall, Campbell grew increasingly frustrated at his inability to prompt Peabody into losing his temper. He felt his campaign ticking away.

When it was time for locals to ask questions, there were the usual eccentrics who wanted to hear themselves talk, give opinions instead of ask questions, and go on and on about personal concerns that worried no one else. The moderators repeatedly had to rein them in to ask a question. But there were also many reasonable queries posed. Through it all, Bo stood composed while Ray appeared increasingly agitated. The latter became especially frustrated with all the precious time lost to folks who enjoyed getting to talk in public and hoped to get quoted in the next morning's *Gazette*.

Elton frequently checked his watch to reassure himself how much time had elapsed without Ray, the moderators, or anyone in the audience mentioning the UFO investigation. Could he have been narcissistic to assume it would play a big role in the debate? With thirty minutes to go, he began to feel relief.

Ray decided he could wait no longer to play what he hoped would be his trump card. None of his attacks had distracted Bo, and he had failed to get another round of applause as big as the one for his opening statement. It was also clear the sheriff's answers were drawing more applause than his own. Since no one was asking about the UFO investigation, he would have to bring it up. So after giving a quick response to an audience member's question about speeding tickets, Ray fired.

"Now, y'all, I would be remiss if I didn't bring up something which typifies the poor leadership of our present Sheriff's Department. It's something that has recently caused our whole community to become the laughingstock of the entire nation," he announced.

The room suddenly became quiet. Elton's stomach tightened and he felt warm. Bo braced himself. Casandra clasped her hands tightly.

"Sheriff Peabody's leadership has reached such a low point that he has even been singled out for ridicule in none other than *The National Exposure*."

There were a few laughs in the audience. Elton hoped some of them were nervous.

"We all know about the now famous lights from a few weeks back. They were spotted in Johnston, Jackson, and Polk Counties. But only the Johnston County Sheriff's Department, led by our very own sheriff, actually even tried chasing down some little green-manned UFO in the woods and, of course, found nothing."

Now there were more laughs. This time they all sounded genuine.

"Nothing, that is, except the sheriff's own brother. Wow. What a strange coincidence, huh? Then the sheriff interviews his brother himself and suddenly shelves the whole investigation."

At the mention of Sheriff Peabody's brother, Elton felt his stomach contract. But how touched he was when his mother and Casandra each simultaneously put a hand on either knee. "Please help us, dear Lord," Elton silently prayed.

"When the good folks in these parts learned how the Jackson and Polk County Sheriff's Departments were investigating their lights," Mr. Campbell continued, "even though we had more than both of them combined, folks here demanded our officials investigate them too. So the sheriff grudgingly agreed to do so. But he still dragged his feet. You see, Bo Peabody only likes to do what he wants to do. And just what has he actually done to find out what those lights really were and to assure the citizens of this county they have nothing to fear from them?"

"Mason, Tammy Jean," Sheriff Peabody interrupted. "Instead of fully answering the voter's question, Mr. Campbell has gone way over his allotted answer time to bring up a whole new set of charges against me. I think I should be allowed to respond."

Several people in the audience seconded his request, and the moderators agreed.

"First of all," the sheriff began, "like Jackson and Polk Counties, our sheriff's department got a slew of phone calls on a recent Friday night concerning strange bright white lights in the sky, which witnesses said were moving too fast and sudden to be planes. Folks were understandably concerned and many of them were downright scared. So, like other area sheriff's departments, we investigated. Fortunately, it was otherwise a slow night. So we could afford to devote several deputies to try to see exactly what was happening. Since I believe in hands-on policing, and I was caught up on paperwork, I went too. Several deputies, concerned citizens, and I saw this extremely bright light deep in the woods west of Cleburne. So we investigated on foot since there was no road access. The closer we got to this light, the brighter it got. Then, with no warning, it vanished. When we got to the clearing where it had been, it was obvious something or somebody had flattened almost everything in the area, there were some burn marks, and some unknown yellow deposits. We took pictures of all this which were released to *The Gazette.*

"Since then, we have interviewed"—he glanced at a notecard—"forty-two residents who reported seeing one or more UFOs that evening. I checked today and that is more than our two neighboring county sheriff's departments combined. And all our witness statements are available to the public. So we have neither dragged our feet on this matter nor covered anything up.

"It's true I've been careful to not let this investigation deter us in the slightest from what I believe are our primary duties of protecting the good people of this county from crime and apprehending criminals. And, though we can't say definitively what those lights were, neither can anybody else. Frankly, if the feds in Washington still can't say what UFOs are, I'm a little skeptical the Johnston County Sheriff's Department with its limited resources can."

This prompted many laughs. With not much time to go, Ray felt himself losing his last chance to score a knockout. So the veteran high school quarterback decided to try to throw a long touchdown pass.

"Bo, you conveniently ignored the fact that the only little green man you found in that clearing just happened to be your own brother. What exactly are you hiding from us about his involvement in all this? This is a classic case of nepotism in government if I've ever seen one. Why don't you reveal what he's told you about all this? Why are you protecting him? Could it be he cooked up this whole light in the woods mystery and you're covering for him? Is that why you delayed a formal investigation?

"Or could it be maybe there's some emotional family matters you don't want exposed and you're therefore selfishly compromising a major investigation, putting your family's desires above the welfare of this county? Is that what *The Exposure* was alluding to and what a lot of folks are speculating about?"

Many gasps were heard and quickly followed by loud boos and hisses. Elton's mother put her hand back on his right knee and now gripped it, as Casandra did with his left. Each told him not to let one word of what they just heard bother him. As ticked off as he was, Elton felt a strange calm come over him. This should be my worst nightmare, he thought. *I've just been publicly ridiculed about the most frightening experience of my life and targeted for public humiliation about my emotional health. Yet it was so meanly done, and the corruption charge so patently false, that I'm not going to let him hurt me,* he reasoned. He was also comforted by the sense that Ray's desperate ploy had backfired. Just how badly would soon be seen.

Bo was so livid he could spit. He thought back to his high school days and realized if someone had said what Ray just did about any of his kin—and in public—he would have beaten him up even if at school, knowing he would be suspended. But he knew what Ray was trying to do. Yet he was not going to let his brother's or his own reputation be defamed like that and before his family, friends, and the whole community. If he did not respond to the charges, and right now, they would fester on end and he would regret it for the rest of his days.

"Ray, it's obvious and frankly pathetic how desperate you are to make something out of absolutely nothing. You're now even having to rely on *The National Exposure* to somehow make your case. Heck, I think most of us would be embarrassed to be on the same side as that rag."

Laughter ensued, along with applause.

"Now, Ray, it's true my brother was in the clearing that night. That light was in the woods directly behind *his* backyard. We got more calls from his neighborhood about strange lights—including the one we followed in the woods—than any other in the county. So Elton, my brother, investigated. Heck, I would have too, if there was a strange big light at night behind my backyard and the dogs were all going wild, and I bet maybe even Ray Campbell might have braved facing some little green men if this had happened in his backyard too."

More laughter rippled across the audience.

"Yes, we did find my brother in that clearing that night, and we talked to him at length about exactly what all he saw and heard. And you and everyone in this room are free to read his full interview with me *and* Deputy Otis Cummings that night. He gave an interview with *The Gazette* that repeated the same account. It was a terrifying experience. Was he shook up about it that night? You bet. I sure would have been. I bet everybody in this room would have been, including Ray Campbell.

"But the very idea I have somehow covered up anything here to protect a family member is garbage. And the nerve of you to imply emotional problems about somebody with no evidence and before a public audience. You should be ashamed, Ray. My brother is a fine teacher and has gone on with his life after this incident, and I'm proud of him and all my family."

The audience roared and Elton felt himself smile. Casandra clapped loudly and exclaimed, "He just hit it right out of the park."

With just ten minutes to go, Ray realized he had almost no cards left to play. He had to do something to get back the momentum he lost with Bo's opening statement. So he did what he had not dared do when thinking rationally. But, distracted by the fact the crowd had clearly turned against him, believing he knew a genuine weakness of his foe, and being too confident of his rival's sense of decency, he would let go one final, desperate throw.

"Bo, I mean no disrespect to you or any of your family. I just think the evidence is clear that you're guilty of favoritism."

"Mr. Campbell, I do hate to interrupt," Mrs. Robards, the co-moderator interjected. "But we only have a few minutes left and there's still a line of folks waiting to ask questions, and y'all agreed this would be the part of the debate when the audience members could ask each of you questions."

Several audience members applauded and a few laughed, enjoying how what had been a pretty gentlemanly debate had gotten a lot more exciting.

"Tammy Jean, I appreciate that. But I believe this is important," Ray declared. "The people need to know how unprofessional this sheriff is in getting rid of his best deputies—good men, all of us—and the only ones with the seasoned experience, expertise, and guts to dare stand up to him and tell him when he's wrong. He got rid of deputies with way more experience than him and replaced us with a bunch of young yes men who'll just do whatever he says."

Now there was a silence made all the more striking by all the recent noise in the audience. Elton was not sure if people actually took this latest attack seriously or if they were eager to see if Bo might lose his famous cool and finally unload on his foe. He also knew the real reason Ray had been fired and wondered if his brother would at long last drop that bomb. Though a big part of him hoped he would, he also looked a few rows over and saw Mrs. Campbell and all three of their daughters, aged fourteen, twelve, and ten.

Sheriff Peabody was incensed. He had spared the reputation of Ray Campbell and the feelings of his wife and young daughters for two years. He had endured all kinds of false rumors about why he had fired Deputy Campbell, his most popular deputy. Yet he had still refused to be remotely fully frank in his public statements about the dismissal, despite the fact Ray had smeared him all over the county.

How often Bo had bitterly reproached himself for not being honest with the public from the start about Ray's endless womanizing. If he had, he might not have even had an opponent in this election. It now galled him more than ever to have this jerk defame him in public, especially when he knew full well the real truth. Though he had doubts about the wisdom of what he was about to say, Beauregard Peabody rationalized it was necessary to clear his name and cut out this ugly cancer of a public pest once and for all.

"Ray, you know exactly why you were fired. Everyone in the Sheriff's Department and a lot of folks in the county courthouse know why you were fired too. I have bent over backward for two years to spare you and your loved ones the humiliation of publicly releasing that information. I don't think you really want to go there."

Before he could catch himself, Mr. Campbell heard himself retort, "I know you can't handle strong colleagues."

That did it, Bo decided. *You asked for this, Ray. And I don't think you'll ever stop your lying and bullying until you are exposed for the fraud you are,* he told himself.

"To the contrary, Ray. I am surrounded by nothing but strong colleagues. Every deputy in the department and everybody else who works there tells me when I'm off-base on something. Heck, you oughta hear my secretary, Miss Cassie, fuss at me sometimes."

There was a burst of more high-pitched laughter this time, with Casandra's chortle the loudest of all. "He just got some more ladies' votes," she laughed to Elton.

"No, Ray. You weren't fired for being a strong character. You were fired because there were many ladies working in the Sheriff's Department and county courthouse who wouldn't walk down the same hall if they saw you on it."

The audience froze. No one said a word or moved. And most eyes were now on Mr. Campbell.

"No, Ray. You were fired because of a twenty-year pattern of totally inappropriate relationships with female county employees. I don't know how you got away with it for so long. But I decided it had to stop because it's wrong, it's totally unprofessional, it's bad for morale, and it had become too big of a distraction for the department and a number of offices in the courthouse next door. And I warned you about it and you lied to me and your behavior continued. And that's why you got fired. And there's a file of documents this thick documenting everything I've just said.

"No, Ray. There are many reasons why not one present deputy or former Sheriff Speaky Stevens supports you. That's because your record speaks for itself."

There was complete silence for many seconds. The ninety-minute clock had long expired on what ended up being the most memorable debate in the history of Johnston County. Casandra turned to Elton and mouthed, "We nailed him." Elton nodded.

Bo stared at Ray. He had waited years for this. Ray glared at him briefly before staring at his own notecards. He looked at the audience and saw everyone looking back expressionless at him. He dared to look at his wife to see her sitting straight, silently weeping. He quickly turned away to avoid seeing his daughters.

At last he turned back to Bo. "I'm proud of my twenty-one years of service in the Sheriff's Department. I did a fine job and was as respected in this community as any other deputy on the entire force. And I've got nothing to apologize for, and certainly not to you," he announced.

There was some hesitant applause in parts of the audience, but it sounded somewhat forced. After another pause, co-moderator Mason T. Phillips announced, "Ladies and gentlemen, it's now time for our candidates' closing statements. By a coin toss, Sheriff Peabody will go first."

Bo found his closing statement notecard prepared by him and Cassie and gave the same version he had rehearsed to both Cassie and Stevie. Though his words matched the card precisely, he barely heard what he was saying. He felt sure he had won the debate, and decisively, but had all kinds of conflicting emotions. Yes, he was thrilled to have performed much better tonight than he had dared hope, and he was pleased not to have exploded in anger at any of Ray's many unfair accusations. He was also confident he had not only just won reelection but permanently destroyed any chance of Ray Campbell ever coming back to challenge him in a rematch. He also felt more confident than ever the whole UFO story had been taken care of, and he was impressed with how maturely the audience had handled it.

But he knew there would be other consequences from his words tonight lasting far beyond this election. He did not dare look anywhere near where the Campbell family sat. He even briefly hesitated looking at his parents, and he wondered if the Rev. Presseau was in the room. Yes, he believed he was completely justified to finally reveal why his rival was fired; yes, he told the truth; yes, he was far more tactful than he had to be—but had it been truly necessary? Had he not already won the debate and way more than likely the election too? Had he been gratuitous? Had he let his emotions overwhelm Christian decency? Would he regret this? Was this a pyrrhic victory?

When he finished, there was plenty of applause, but it did not sound as enthusiastic as some of the earlier rounds in his favor. Bo did not know if the audience was disappointed in his publicly confirming the rumors most had heard or if people were still processing everything that had just been said and were eager to hear Ray's final comments of the evening.

Ray Campbell made no reference to the preceding drama. Instead, he read his closing statement almost verbatim. He tried to make eye contact with the audience but kept losing his place when he did. So he finally stopped trying and quickly rushed through the rest of what was written on the card. When he finished, there was polite applause, but most people sensed it was largely out of sympathy. The pockets of loud clapping and whistles seemed decidedly forced.

Bo walked over and stuck out his hand, but Ray ignored him and walked into the audience to be surrounded by several supporters, a few of whom hugged him. Bo was mobbed by a much larger crowd who told him how he had completely creamed his foe. Bo thanked them all. He felt very tired and wished it was election night and all this was behind him, hoping he would never have such an election fight again. He also recalled what Mayor Simpson had told him a couple of weeks back about his having to be just as much of a politician as the mayor if he wanted to keep his job. He believed he was right to say what he had that night, and he did feel a big weight had fallen from him, but he felt no joy. Instead, he felt a little dirty and plenty sad at the ugliness of what had happened and so bad for Mrs. Campbell and the Campbell girls. And he felt something for Ray Campbell he never imagined: pity.

12
CHAPTER

The attitude around the county was that the sheriff's election was decided a week early. It was as if Sheriff Peabody's hounds had already treed the fox, and the affair was all over except the shooting. When Friday's *Gazette* ran an article featuring four unnamed female county employees claiming to have been sexually harassed by former Deputy Campbell, the first edition sold out before noon and a special second edition sold out that evening.

The public reaction to the article was a Rorschach test. Many readers took a special delight reading what they were certain was Ray Campbell's professional obituary. They had long resented the popular deputy sitting high and mighty with his family as a deacon in the First Baptist Church on Sunday while secretly gallivanting around the county with so many women the rest of the week. It had been an unexpected thrill when the sheriff finally exposed his disgraced ex-deputy's double life in the debate, and *The Gazette* expose was a deliciously sweet dessert.

Campbell's supporters were angry that it appeared the local establishment had come down so hard on their candidate, but also saddened at the ugly truth exposed. Many were also bitter Campbell had betrayed their trust.

The many apolitical readers either enjoyed the rare dose of local scandal in *The Gazette* or turned the page to the next article.

Others who had heard the rumors for years asked what the big deal was.

But a significant sector of the county viewed the whole matter with sadness. It was as if their idyllic community had been revealed to be replete with the same type of scandal they had always deplored in national politics.

The only reaction unifying all was sympathy for kind Mrs. Campbell and the three Campbell children. And with each thought, lament, and prayer for the family, sympathy for Ray evaporated a little more.

Bo's family wished the whole matter could have remained hidden, but no one faulted him for exposing Ray, who they all saw as a lying, selfish bully—terrible sins in the Peabody worldview. Elton was grateful to Bo for defending his honor and that of the whole family. He reflected how he and his brother had grown closer than ever the last few weeks. Perhaps that made this entire recent drama almost worthwhile—almost.

On election night, Sheriff Peabody's strongest supporters met at Mr. Allen's Grill to watch the election returns on the local TV station hosted by Mason T. Phillips and Tammy Jean Robards. Though everyone at the restaurant felt sure they would win, it was still exciting to get official confirmation, and the lopsided margin of victory was even greater than expected.

When Bo had officially won, everyone cheered and Mr. Allen presented the sheriff with a special blueberry victory pie. Sheriff Peabody thanked all his supporters, especially each of his family members, Miss Cassie, and all the deputies. Then a local black blues band started playing and the tables were pushed against the wall for dancing to ensue. Stevie got Bo to boogie some, and the crowd roared at the big man's moves. This was one of the greatest nights of his life, vindicating all the long hours devoted to molding the Sheriff's Department into the significantly improved law enforcement institution it had become. He had just won what local politicians said was typically the toughest reelection fight he would ever face, the first one, and by a tremendous margin. The queasiness he felt after the debate had abated, and he relished his new-found lack of worry about reelection. Indeed, he was thoroughly enjoying a new four-year smile.

Mr. and Mrs. Peabody were quietly proud of their middle child and so grateful the long and sometimes unpleasant campaign was at last over, and victoriously so. They had been worried about what their second son would do professionally if he lost and dreaded the prospect of his family moving away from Cleburne and their not seeing their only grandchildren nearly as often.

Casandra, Kenley, Elton's sister Melody, and even his long-time student, Penelope Breen, all tried to drag Elton onto the dance floor, but he demurred. He knew better than anyone what a pronounced case of Caucasian rhythm he had, and he had lately become more determined than ever to avoid public embarrassment.

Elton fervently hoped his brother's resounding reelection marked the close of a particularly painful period. He wanted to believe they had all been far too worried and this should be taken as a lesson for him to just try to relax. He took stock and concluded he should be much more appreciative of just how well his life was going. He had struggled through the second most difficult chapter of his life and done pretty well. He had met all his responsibilities at school and faced the inevitable jokes without flinching. He had even stood up to mean Mr. Sneed. And despite all the press coverage and other unwanted attention, he had not let any of it break him. *Hey,* he thought, *I survived being on the front page of the leading national scandal sheet, as well as having my mental stability questioned in a local public forum, and people have still not ostracized me.* In fact, not only had each of the dearest folks in his life been supportive, but he had been touched by all the people he had never imagined caring about him who sought him out to express their concern. Best of all, he reasoned, was that he was a lot stronger than he had been all those years before. Indeed, his sense of unfocused anxiety was not nearly as bad, and he was sleeping better with fewer nightmares.

So he resolved to stop waiting to feel better. Instead, he would try to jumpstart himself out of the cautious crisis mode he had been in for weeks and get on with the life he wanted. In accordance with his newfound sense of well-being, Elton decided he was ready to date again. While he had long been comfortable talking with women and enjoyed many female friends, he had always been uncomfortable with romantic relationships. The confident-appearing showman of a lecturer had little assurance on the dating front. His perception was that everything he did was being judged, and he could rarely relax. Unable to imagine someone being attracted to him, dates were exhausting performances where he was always on, trying to entertain, be witty, or endlessly interesting. He was convinced he had to earn any affection.

But it was the sexual aspects of dating which most unnerved him. No matter how hard he tried, he was never able to edit out of his mind all the seemingly endless biblical scriptures condemning any sex outside of marriage. How he envied most folks' ability to do so with ease. He sometimes wished he had not been reared in such a religious, Bible-influenced, church-going family. Perhaps, if he were only secular, dating would not be such a challenge. It was not hard for him to get dates, but tough to keep going out with the same lady for very long. Elton was even afraid to provide the first kiss. Once, an exasperated date at his house asked for a glass of water so she could take a birth control pill. He figured that might be a sign. He suspected girls soon stopped going out with him because he would not make a move on them. But he also wondered if they were frustrated he did not seem able to relax and stop performing.

The few girlfriend relationships he had had were all disappointing. While most of the ladies were sweet, he always felt he had to shield them from just how anxious he felt or they would leave. Two of the three he had dared confide in about his past mental problems left him soon afterward. He was particularly disappointed with one since he had been supportive of her trying to deal with the death of her mother many years before.

He figured his girlfriends likely sensed he was not secure enough to marry. When he confessed to one how he had never had a desire to, she told him the thought of life without a husband and children was "terrifying" and that dating someone with whom there was no chance of marriage was "a waste of time." Not long afterward, when breaking up with him over the phone, he could only recall her last sentence: "You're *so* sad." He thought he had hidden it and concluded he needed to throw himself further into the performance mode.

With none of his girlfriends had he ever felt a special bond of friendship like he had with Beryl. While attracted to them physically, he had yet to find one with the same interests or personality type. And he had never come close to finding anyone he saw as a "soul mate."

Once, when lamenting his few and frustrating girlfriend experiences, Beryl tried to buck up Elton's spirits.

"Well, as a wise old Hebrew once told me"—his Jewish shrink— "you can't possibly know what you want in a woman, much less what you really need, until you've had at least five serious relationships," Beryl announced.

"Well, since I've had exactly three romances lasting longer than a month, perhaps there's still hope," Elton replied.

He smiled at the time he shared that wisdom with a Korean student in the throes of a rough breakup. She had cried to Mr. Peabody after class how she had lost "the love of my life."

He first tried reassuring her she would be pretty freaky to have already met Mr. Right at seventeen. Then he relayed how a wise old Jewish gentleman said she would need at least five serious relationships with men before knowing what she really needed romantically.

"Oh, no! I can't have my heart broken five times. I'll die of heartbreak," she wailed, which led Mr. Peabody to conclude Beryl's shrink's love advice might not be ideal with students.

Reviewing his own history, Elton acknowledged he had known some very nice young ladies with whom he enjoyed discussing literature, film, politics, and other common interests, but they always had a beau or were not physically attractive to him. Yet when he tried to develop a romance with a couple of the latter who were substantive, fun, and really fond of him, it had never worked out, and he felt terrible breaking things off.

So he was relieved Bo married and had children and Melody had enjoyed several long-term relationships and would surely marry and have children as well. No one had ever pressured Elton to have a family. The consensus was he was too sensitive a loner. Indeed, his mother never encouraged dating for fear he could be hurt.

But there remained something exciting about a first date, though he had no hope of anything lasting ever coming of it. How he wished Kenley was not already taken. She had seemed to be his ideal combination of beauty, ebullience, character, and common interests. Heck, she was the first gal he had ever known who even shared his fascination with UFOs. And she was a swell writer whose articles chronicling Cleburne's Friday night lights had been riveting. He hoped she had broken up with her boyfriend now that she had settled into a new town. But when they met for lunch at the Purple Thumb again, his dream of taking her to dinner and a film that Friday were dashed when it came out she remained hitched to her beau. *We still live in a fallen world indeed,* he concluded.

But his dating world had not completely collapsed. Kimberly McSweeney was a fine-looking, twenty-something brunette staffer in the County Records Department who he had enjoyed chatting with on occasion. The courthouse building where she worked was conveniently next to the Sheriff's Department. He had thought about asking her out for some time but was not sure if they knew each other well enough. Yet he was tired of his UFO funk and figured he could use an absorbing distraction. So he made a point of running several errands near and in the courthouse, conveniently walking by the records department to speak to Kimberly just before the twelve-noon lunch break. Since her face appeared to light up when he said hello and they made pleasant small talk, he asked if she would like to join him for lunch downtown. She immediately agreed and they ate together near the courthouse. Though doubtful about how much they had in common, Elton was quite taken with her looks: a pretty face with an impressive figure who dressed stylishly. Plus, she was polite and seemed interested in him. So he dared to ask her out on a date for Friday evening, and she said yes.

Now he had something to be excited about the rest of the week. Though he figured reality would inevitably intrude, he nevertheless enjoyed the sense of possibility and still fantasized about her. When he picked her up for dinner, her hair was thick and long, and she wore a red shirt with a white skirt and heels. He told her how lovely she looked, and she seemed flattered. Elton took her to Cleburne's one Thai restaurant, which he adored and she had never tried, Thai One On. They had a leisurely dinner in which the conversation revolved around their favorite foods, likes and dislikes at work, and dating history, with Elton's brief and full of funny anecdotes. Then they were off to see a local movie.

Of all people, who did he see in the theatre lobby but Penelope Breen who immediately widened her eyes and grinned at him. He did not recognize the man on her arm and, as soon as her date got in line at the concession stand, Miss Breen went straight for Elton.

"Hey, Mr. Peabody. Who's your friend?"

After introductions, Kimberly went to the ladies' room and Penelope wasted no time.

"So she's a hottie."

"Thank you, dear. Who's your date?"

"Oh, he's just some guy from the college I know. My heart's still reserved for you."

"Stop it, Penelope. He looks like a nice young man, and it's refreshing to see one clean-cut and well dressed."

"So how serious are you and this Miss Kimberly?"

"We're friendly acquaintances."

"Oh. How friendly?" She smiled and winked.

"Please. For the record, this is our first date."

"Woohoo, Mr. Peabody. So tonight's a big night. Be sure to play your cards right."

"You never quit, do you? Everything has to be reduced to something sexual."

Laughing and thoroughly enjoying herself, she remarked, "Well, don't get too friendly with her. Remember to save yourself for me. I'm still saving myself for you."

"Enough. Do you talk this way to other teachers, or am I the only one accorded this 'honor?'"

With Penelope laughing too hard to talk, Elton introduced himself to her date who had just returned with soda and popcorn.

When Kimberly returned, Penelope immediately declared, "We should double date sometime."

"Make a swell evening, kids. Pleased to meet you, Sam. Bye," Elton said as he led his date into the theatre. Though he would never go out with her, he did secretly enjoy Penelope's flirtations. Having taught thousands of students for over a decade, she was a minority of one in many fun respects. Part of him would love to ideally date her, yet all his instincts told him such a relationship was without hope and would ruin the innocent chemistry they enjoyed. But when she graduated soon, he knew he would miss her and hoped she would stay in touch.

The movie would have been a bore without a date to make witty remarks to during the dry scenes and enjoy her laughter. Since Kimberly had shared her love of dogs over dinner, Elton asked if she would like to meet General Longstreet after the film. So they went to his house where the general was thrilled to meet someone new. She was delighted with him and eagerly agreed to help with the evening ritual of letting him in the backyard to play fetch the tennis ball. When they got back inside, they sat on the sofa and continued chatting. All was going well from Elton's perspective. In fact, he wanted to try to kiss her when she suddenly changed topics.

"So this is where your UFO adventure began, right?" She leaned toward him and, for the first time, appeared excited.

Surprised, he simply nodded his head and wondered what had inspired such a swift subject shift. At no time had the topic been raised before by either. While he had not felt a strong connection with her, he wanted to read her heretofore laidback demeanor as emotionally secure maturity. He had just been grateful for the lack of conversational lulls.

"I'd just love to hear all about it, and straight from you," she continued. Elton just tried to smile.

"So was there a real spaceship? And did you actually go inside? Did you see any aliens? And what were they like?"

His mood moved into another orbit. It was as if he had been seduced by an intoxicating character on stage, only to meet the actress playing her backstage after the show to find her an entirely different person.

"I didn't see any ship or aliens or, if I did, I didn't know it. I have no memory of going inside anything. I know it was the scariest experience of my life and then I blacked out and got discovered by the sheriff's party."

"That is so awesome," she enthused and continued to ask questions.

"Kimberly, there's really nothing else to tell. I wish it had never happened," he said softly. But she was convinced there was still so much more to share.

"There are so many folks who I would love to share your story with, including my family," she exclaimed. Elton quietly sighed.

"Everything's in that *Gazette* story from a few Sundays back," he volunteered. Looking at the general, Elton beckoned him over.

"Yeah, but how about the real skinny? I can't believe you told them everything. Are you really telling me there was no flying saucer or space aliens? If you want, I promise I won't tell. I'm just dying to know what really happened," she gushed.

Elton massaged the back of his dog's ears and got lost in how content and satisfied General Longstreet appeared. He was glad Miss Penelope spotted him at the movie house and now judged their conversation to be the highlight of the evening. As for his date, at least he had gotten a good dinner, a halfway decent film, and a couple of days of looking forward to going out with a good looker. He informed her he had developed a headache and asked if she minded him taking her home. She was polite but, for the first time in their relationship, there were gaps in their conversation on the drive back to her house, so much so that Elton turned on the radio in lieu of trying to fill the silence.

When he got to her home, he did not walk her to the door or lean over to kiss her goodbye. She thanked him for a fun evening and he wished her well. On the way back he did not think for a long time, lost in a tired, quiet world all his own. Just when he had dared hope the biggest, most awful light of his life was finally extinguished, it flickered back to life. Was he ultimately just the UFO man to people who had not known him well before last month? Was this the rest of his life?

Would he ever find closure with this matter? Though he had not wanted to admit it, tonight's disappointment reminded him he still had a general sense of unease about the whole business. To be sure, it was not nearly as rough as it had been but, in a real sense, he had never felt more alone, not even in the mental hospital. At least there he had doctors, nurses, and other patients with whom he had to interact each day. In fact, except while sleeping in his room, he was virtually never by himself. But now, even when surrounded by thirty students in a classroom, he had a psychic itch no one could scratch. And even if someone could, he did not even know where it was.

He wondered if he should see a shrink again. A couple had been helpful at the time of his breakdown. But who could help him with this? Should he go on the Internet in search of some *psychiatrist with UFO experience*? How could anyone identify with what he had seen and felt ever since? Who would even believe him? Could his mind have tricked him? Was he a lot more mentally ill than he thought? Was his family right to see him as so fragile?

Or maybe he was long overdue to just man up. Everyone had all kinds of traumatic experiences: terrible car wrecks, cancer, sudden deaths of family members. He had had nothing that bad. He did not even have a scratch from his big drama. *Yet the minute some hot chick gets real curious about my big story—maybe the only reason she went out with me—I go into a funk? Heck, maybe I could have bedded her on the promise of some green alien-enhanced sex. What a moron.* He sighed.

Yet he felt a deep sadness and separation from everyone and yearned for it all to make sense. How he longed for the threads of his incredible experience to be sewn up to provide meaning and understanding. *Dear God, will you please at least give me a clue?*

CHAPTER 13

Elton had delayed talking with the Rev. Charles Presseau because he did not want to relive his experience, he wanted to believe he was tough enough to not need pastoral counseling this time, and he dreaded what his minister might say. He cringed at the possibility of being told this was a religious experience which he must examine or, more likely and much worse, yet another mystery which he would just have to live with and *have faith* about.

But it had been two months since his unexplained encounter and, though entirely functional—at least to the world—he remained emotionally as well as intellectually discombobulated. He had always known it was far easier to create a great illusion than a great reality. And since his pastor had been so kind and supportive of him and his entire family when he had his nervous breakdown, he figured it was worth trying to talk with him again.

It was a late Friday afternoon in May when Elton was warmly greeted by the Rev. Presseau in his First Presbyterian Church office. The minister came around his large desk so he could sit in a chair next to his visitor. He was a sixty-something who had pastored the church for over twenty years. Elton had always been fond of him for how cheerful he was to everyone, regardless of the circumstances, and because he preached sermons which were thoughtful and comforting enough to sit through all the boring hymns and announcements to get to them. His prayers during worship services always struck him as particularly well crafted, sincere, and heartfelt. The pastor had a glowing reputation and was one of the most widely respected folks in the county. Elton's family adored him.

After opening small talk, the Rev. Presseau asked how he could assist him. Elton was touched by how eagerly the man appeared to want to help, which made it easier to unburden himself. Though it was hard to start, he appreciated the minister did not try to speak for him or fill in the silent spaces.

"Pastor, I've had a very tough time figuring out how to deal with what I went through a couple of months back with my *UFO experience* or whatever it actually was. I've been able to just about finish out the school year now, and pretty much everything is back to normal. I'm so grateful Bo won reelection and the important people in my life have been real supportive of me. I'm going through my regular routines but... I just feel so unanswered. I don't even know what the right questions are. I've tried and tried so hard and so often to explain what I saw, heard, and felt that night, but I don't know anything more today than I did two months ago. And I've tried to avoid thinking about it, hoping perhaps my subconscious mind would provide answers, but I still get nothing. I've read more about other people who've had similarly strange experiences, and mine still doesn't make sense. Nobody I've talked with can answer me, either.

"I prayed so hard to God that awful night to save me, and I guess He did since here I am and completely unharmed too, at least physically. But I just don't know how to detect any answers from Him about what happened and why and what I should do or think about it. I can't believe it was angels or His way of trying to send me a message. If it was, then I guess I'm just too thick to get it.

"Worst of all, I feel more alone and lonelier than ever. I still have this general sense of unease that I can't shake. And I feel like it's all so meaningless. I don't know what my purpose is. Each year this time another crop of students graduates, but I remain. They all move away, start families, and move forward with their lives, but I remain stuck. Here. Feeling I should be doing more or something else, but I don't know what.

"You were so good to me and my whole family the last time I spoke with you when I was struggling. So I figured I'd ask your advice about this. Thanks for your time and listening."

As the young man stared at the floor or bookshelves while speaking, the older one studied his face and listened intently. When Elton had said his piece, sighed, and shifted in his chair, the minister looked out the window at the trees and flower garden in full bloom. He looked at the floor briefly and then spoke.

"Elton, you are a remarkable young gentleman. I've known you the majority of your life. I've seen a shy young fellow struggle through the inevitably difficult period of adolescence and always succeed in school and remain a good Christian. Like so many folks in graduate school, or any extremely challenging, transitional phase of life, you hit quite a rough patch. But you not only got through it, you completed your degree and went on to become an extremely well respected and even beloved teacher. Principal Toombs and so many students have told me what a fine job you've done steering the school's Presbyterian Club too. Indeed, you've been an excellent role model for quite a few young people in our community, and I'm right proud of you, Elton."

"Thank you, Reverend."

"Two months ago you had an experience for which you had no preparation—an amazing, incredible, and terribly frightening ordeal for which neither you nor anyone else has definitive answers to any of your entirely understandable questions. You have been quite shaken and sought answers from a variety of quarters, and yet there are still no answers."

Pausing to lean forward and lowering his voice, the minister continued, "Elton, with all my heart, son, I so wish I could give you every answer you so desperately seek. But I'm just a pastor. Though I know you saw something remarkable that night, I cannot say what it was.

"But I am a student of the Bible, and I do have some life experience and observations to share which I hope will be of help. First, God teaches us to be grateful for all the many blessings He has bestowed upon us. As terrifying and disturbing as this bizarre incident was, you were never alone, Elton. God was with you in that clearing. As Hebrews 13:5 teaches us, 'be content with such things as ye have: for he hath said, I will never leave thee, nor forsake thee' and, as Isaiah 41:10 tells us, 'Fear thou not; for I am with thee: be not dismayed; for I am thy God: I will strengthen thee; yea, I will help thee; yea, I will uphold thee with the right hand of my righteousness.' As awful an experience as you had, Elton, God not only protected you but shielded you from any physical harm. He sent your own fine brother and several deputies to rescue you.

"And for all the understandable difficulties you've had trying to make this experience comprehensible—as any of us would have had—you have, to paraphrase William Faulkner, not merely endured, but prevailed. Yes, I'm sure there were many times when you wanted to stay in bed and not face it all again, but you went right back to work and faced all those folks who I'm sure wanted to know all about your experience—and you triumphed, Elton. Was it tough? You bet. But what in life isn't tough that's truly worth achieving?

"So now you realize life has gone on and the crisis is over, but you still yearn for what it all means, how to fit all these confusing pieces of the puzzle together. Yet as my French cousins say, 'C'est la vie.' Such is life. All life is a mystery. We know nothing for certain. Our faith in God is just that—faith. But faith is a powerful and wonderful thing. It can move mountains. And just look what your faith has gotten you, Elton. You have faced something that almost no one has ever faced, and look how extraordinarily well you have handled it too. Your faith and hard work have made you a much stronger person than you were all those years ago when you were faced with another great challenge, and you triumphed over that as well.

"So I have faith you will continue to weather the inevitable questions bound to accompany such an experience and that you will continue to meet all your responsibilities. This is an inevitable challenge of life. None of us knows the answers. But we have our wonderful guidebook, the Bible, to help show us the way. And God loves us all more than we can ever know. The Bible teaches us to give God our troubles and to be joyful.

"So you don't have to figure it out, Elton. Not now, next year, nor perhaps ever in this lifetime. And that's all right, son. *We don't have to figure it all out.* And thank the Good Lord for that.

"So I encourage you to try your best to drown in the positive. When you get those anxious thoughts or feelings, dwell in all the many rich blessings thy Father has bestowed upon thee. Remind thyself how strong and capable thee are and recall God is always by thy side. Always. He doesn't expect you to have all the answers. Not remotely.

"And, probably not now, but one day I expect you will come to appreciate your unique experience. You may even want to write or lecture about it, which I recommend if you think that would help. I hope and I believe you will one day take great comfort in the fact that, in the most terrifying moments of your life, God got you through them without a scratch. And I find it very difficult to believe you will ever again experience anything remotely like the terror you felt that night. What a comfort it should be that you have already likely faced your most frightening experience and got through it in one piece. Faith in God, Elton."

"Thank you, Pastor. I appreciate what you're saying. It's good for me to hear it."

"Let's have prayer, Elton," the minister said as he put one hand on the young Peabody's back and the other on his own bent head. Elton bowed his head and clasped his hands.

"Gracious God, we thank thee, oh Lord, for all thy bountiful blessings. Thou art a loving and generous God, and we should always be grateful. Thank you, Lord, for all the guidance and help you have provided your faithful servant Elton Peabody. Thank you for helping him through such a uniquely challenging period of his life, for protecting and inspiring him to carry on when his burden felt so heavy, for giving him strength to persevere and move forward. Please continue to guide him, Heavenly Father, to provide him with peace of mind, to reassure him he is not responsible for knowing remotely all things, to comfort him when he is weary and confused, and to minister to him when he is afraid and in pain. Please reassure him he is loved deeply by you and is never alone, that thou art with us always. We ask all this in the name of the Father, the Son, and the Holy Spirit. Amen."

Elton Peabody felt the most relaxed he had felt in a very long time. It was as if he were floating in a sea of calm. Nothing seemed urgent. Items in the pastor's study unnoticed when he entered now appeared to sparkle. Indeed, the sense of vague but pronounced unease carried into the office seemed to have been lifted. On one hand, not a single question had been answered. But now it no longer seemed to matter nearly as much. How he yearned to stay in that moment forever. Perhaps he had tried to over-intellectualize this whole thing and should just be grateful for all the very many real blessings he enjoyed and dive deeper into life. How often he had had that thought during so many past trials. Alas, his life had taught him this was a resolution light years' easier to make than to create into a reality.

He shook hands with and thanked his minister who smiled and gave him a hug. Elton almost choked up from the realization there were people in his life who cared about him very much and thought so well of him.

Before he left, the pastor gave a final piece of advice: "Elton, lose yourself in service."

14

The general unease endured since his encounter remained. But it did not weigh as much. Elton was able to focus better, and not just on work. He tried harder to appreciate all his blessings and how very much better he was now than in March, April, or even before his talk with the Rev. Presseau. Yes, he still was not back to where he had been before the incident, but he was confident at least no one could tell.

Indeed, the school year had turned out exceedingly well. As he had in past periods of super stress, he channeled his anxiety through his lectures to be more dramatic, physical, and funny than usual. His students could be forgiven for thinking their history teacher's UFO encounter had infused him with even more energy than before.

Penelope had jokingly asked after a class, "So what did those little green men give you aboard that UFO, Mr. Peabody?"

Though the unease always returned, he still got a rush during most lectures which remained for at least a while afterward. It was when the depression got especially bad that his lectures suffered. That was when it was such a struggle to focus, avoid speaking in a monotone, and remember all he wanted to say. But he had worked hard that spring to outrun the depressive fog that was ever near and took some satisfaction from having mostly succeeded.

He was also grateful the vast majority of students, staffers, teachers, and even educrats had treated him no differently since his encounter. If some gossiped about him, he did not want to know. He was particularly appreciative of Principal Bob Toombs standing by him without reservation, and he was relieved his long-time foe, Mr. Sneed, had either been unsuccessful in his efforts to derail him or simply unconcerned.

As with every other *crisis* in his life, he figured his own innate anxiety grossly exaggerated a slew of potential threats arising from his big encounter. *As always,* he concluded, *I am my only threat. Why can't I just realize that and relax?*

The end of the spring term finished all right. As usual, no matter how scrupulously Mr. Peabody tried to prepare for every possible hiccup, the pace was more frenetic than usual. But he was quite honored that more students than ever before visited his classroom to say how much they had enjoyed his class, and many seniors who had taken him more than once remarked he was their best teacher ever. He got many handshakes, hugs, and a peck on the cheek from Penelope. He was happy for her to finally soon be a college student and not just date them.

"But just say the word, Mr. Peabody, and I'll travel the whole wide world with you. Just you, me, and nobody and nothing else— not even any little green men." She giggled.

He could not help but laugh as they stood alone in his classroom after his last class on the last day of the school year. She was one of the students he hoped would stop by to say goodbye and was touched she did.

"So from now on I'm calling you 'Elton.'" She smiled. "Or maybe I'll be the only one in your life who can just call you 'Elt.'" She laughed.

He chuckled and hoped he was not blushing. In spite of all her inappropriate comments, including sometimes in class, he knew he would miss her and hoped she would visit.

As appreciative as he was of so many compliments this time of year, and as much as he looked forward to the far more laid-back summer, graduation remained a poignant marker. He still imagined another class of young people going out into the world to embark on a variety of exciting adventures while he remained in little Cleburne, still teaching high school history. Yes, he had done far more with his life than he dared dream when he was such an awkward, shy boy growing up, or could imagine twelve years ago, but each graduation made him feel like his life was still stuck in second gear while everyone else was shifting into third. And he worried the increased amount of free time in the summer could make it tougher to put the incident on a back burner.

The first Sunday in June started the annual spate of June weddings. Roscoe Peabody, a first cousin, was getting married in mid-afternoon at the First Presbyterian Church. Driving several counties over for the occasion were Elton's Aunts Altoona and Minnie Lou, his father's retired big sisters. Elton especially enjoyed their company since they were not only eternally sweet but two of the least pretentious people he had ever been privileged to know. That helped explain their often unintentional hilarity. They had arrived at the Peabody home that morning to ride to church with Joshua and Ruth since they were fond of the Rev. Presseau. Minnie Lou thought he was an exceptionally spiritual gentleman, Altoona thought he was exceptionally handsome, and both said he preached a far sight better sermon than their own pastor.

They were grateful the Rev. Presseau always remembered them and gave each a hug after the worship service. Then the entire family went to the home place for its weekly lunch together. Following the meal, Ruth told her sisters-in-law that their niece, Melody, had recently visited her local Unitarian Universalist Church.

"Oh, child. Now that's one of them places where folks get confused," Minnie Lou warned.

"But everyone there was real nice," Melody tried to reassure her. "It was most interesting too. Some parts of the worship service were like ours and some weren't. One big difference was the Unitarian Church has a lady pastor."

At that, Altoona shook her head. "A woman ain't got no business in the pulpit," she corrected.

"Oh, Aunt Altoona. Why not? I go to a lady gynecologist," Melody stated.

"And a woman ain't got no business down there, neither," Altoona replied.

Chuckling and wanting to quickly change topics, Joshua told Minnie Lou how pretty her scarf looked. Melody gave her father a knowing grin.

"Oh, sweet Melody gave me this for my birthday. I'm right proud of it too. Thank you, darling."

Ruth asked her sisters-in-law if they were excited about Cousin Roscoe's wedding that afternoon.

"Oh, Ruth. That's a sore subject," Altoona answered.

"What in the world do you mean, Altoona?" Ruth asked.

"Well," Altoona responded, "after you and Joshua's Sunday school class this morning—you know, we so like y'all's teacher, Mr. Roberts. That man truly knows the Good Book. And, Ruth, what's a fine-looking man like that still single at his age? He must be knocking on sixty by now. Oh, but that poor Elrod Rogers. That man is so kind, but dog if he ain't ugly as sin. When the Good Lord was handing out looks, poor Mr. Elrod was at the back of the line. Bless his heart. When he fell down the ugly tree, dog if he didn't hit every branch. Gracious alive, he got hit upside the head with a great big old ugly stick. But he somehow hitched hisself a wife. Oh, I wonder what she looks like. Well, if Mr. Elrod can, I don't know why Mr. Roberts can't. Well. What was I saying? Oh, but before I get to the wedding situation—I'll get to that directly—did you see Ethel Lynn Talbot this morning? Joshua, she has aged badly."

"Ain't that the gospel truth," Minnie Lou added. "The poor woman's hair is now snow white."

"She ain't dying it no more." Her brother smiled.

"And when did she get to be such a great big old fat thing? Anyway, I'm coming to your question, Ruth, about why Minnie Lou and I may not be at the wedding," Altoona declared.

"Miss the wedding?" Ruth gasped.

"Well, now hear me out, sister-in-law. After Sunday school, all these sweet ladies from y'all's class kept coming up to me. And at first I was right touched 'cause I thought they just wanted to see and speak to me. But, oh no. Every one of them kept saying, 'Oh, Altoona. We are so sorry to hear about Miss Minnie Lou.' Well, I had absolutely no idea what all them women were talking about. But I didn't want to look stupid, so I just nodded and said, 'Oh, well, thank you. It'll all work out.' And then they'd say, 'Well, we are sure going to add your sister to our prayer list,' to which I said, 'Oh, thank you. That's mighty kind of you.' And then I really perked up when some of 'em started saying how they sure understood if we weren't able to make it to the wedding this afternoon. Well, that's when I realized Minnie Lou must have sure given them one heck of a fine story."

"Minnie Lou, what in the world's the matter?" Ruth asked.

Minnie Lou Peabody looked slightly uncomfortable and unsure of what to say.

"Tell 'em, Minnie Lou. Now come on," Altoona insisted.

"Well, I said I wasn't feeling the best and was trying to take sick," she replied.

"Oh, you did not," Altoona corrected. "Say what you told them nice people."

"Well, I don't know. I just indicated I might not feel up to going to the wedding is all," Minnie Lou declared.

"Joshua, your sister told all them fine folks she had a brain tumor."

"Oh, my Lord, Minnie Lou! Is that true?" Ruth implored.

"No! She ain't bit more got no more brain tumor than General Longstreet," Altoona announced.

Trying to keep from laughing, Joshua asked, "Well, sister, why did you tell 'em you did?"

After a pause, Minnie Lou confided, "Well. It just sounded so much better than hemorrhoids."

CHAPTER 15

Ten weeks after his life-altering encounter, Elton Peabody continued to become more at peace with or at least resigned about it, but much unfocused anxiety remained, now aggravated by the additional free time he enjoyed or endured each summer. He had always taught summer school out of concern—fear, really—that too many task-less hours tended to spike his stress level. For this summer, in particular, he believed he needed to be preoccupied with work and whatever else would keep his general anxiety at an acceptable level. Yes, talking with the Rev. Presseau, everyone else's support, and just time had all helped, but he knew he was not fully back to normal, and none of his original questions about the incident had been answered.

Mr. Peabody enjoyed teaching both the academically strongest students and many of the weakest in his summer classes, at least those with a decent attitude. Johnston County High teachers could volunteer to teach up to two classes each summer, as opposed to their standard five in the fall and spring. In both his summer classes were many of the school's star pupils who wanted to graduate early to go on to college—what's the rush? thought Elton—as well as many who had failed a history class during the regular academic year. Many of the best students had taken Mr. Peabody's other history classes, and several were favorites of his. It was a lot easier and more fun teaching the better students too. They were more enthusiastic learners, he could cover more material with them, they were better able and more willing to participate in class discussions, they wrote far better essays that did not take so long to mark up with corrections and comments, and he did not have to finesse how to massage delivering poor test or term paper grades so as not to demoralize the students and possibly their parents too. Plus, the stronger students got more of his jokes.

But Elton made an extra effort to excite the students who had failed history during the regular school year. He knew how utterly boring most history teachers were. In fact, so many at his school were physical education instructors with a free period or two to fill. While educrats would never dream of putting a PE teacher in charge of an English or math class, they were convinced anyone could teach social studies. Thus, many PE teachers did despite not having a history or even a social studies degree. Mr. Peabody had nothing against people with PE degrees teaching PE classes, but never understood how they could also teach history classes when the educrats would never imagine letting him or any of the social science faculty teach a PE course. Elton was fully aware of sorry excuses for history teachers having their students take turns reading aloud from the textbook during each class. He also knew of other "history" teachers having their classes watch films of the school's latest football and basketball games. Truly, he lamented, the social sciences are the academic ghetto of secondary schools.

So Mr. Peabody was determined to deliver his very best performances to inspire students to take interest in their heritage. It was quite rewarding to have summer students who had failed due to being utterly bored by a loser instructor and excite them with how fascinating and engrossing our past really is. It was a special joy to ignite a hidden spark that would light up a whole new world of academic interest and ability in students that would hopefully bear fruit long after the summer. Elton saw the task of trying to motivate students whom the schools had failed to be one of his greatest professional duties.

This summer he was gratified to energize many heretofore failing students. As always, there were some who were already beyond reach. But at least they had a positive enough attitude to be in summer school and make some effort, however small. And Elton treasured the smaller classes which were more conducive to discussion, had far fewer tests and papers to grade, and benefitted from the generally more laidback vibe of summer school.

Even the normally uber uptight disciplinary principal, the infamous Frank Sneed, was noticeably less anal retentive in the summer. Elton had studiously avoided the disciplinarian's presence ever since their last unpleasant meeting right after his big incident, and he was grateful for no further confrontations with the jerk. He resolved to continue taking pains to avoid him since experience had repeatedly confirmed no one's personality changes—ever. So why go near a negative one?

Still, despite how well the summer had started, Elton acknowledged three less classes and no Presbyterian Club meetings had invited an uptick of unwanted thoughts about that fated Friday in March. *What to do now?* he asked. He was sick of rewinding the whole incident in his mind and trying to reasonably arrive at answers. He no longer asked God for understanding. Instead, he just continued to plea for peace of mind or acceptance of the unknowable. He had told his story to all those closest to him, and none had any more answers than he did and not nearly as many questions. *So what now?* he kept repeating. *Is there nothing I can do to try to get some closure? Must I continue to endure this chronic unease forever?*

There was one possibility that had been slowly boiling on his back burner for some time. He had not dared broach it with any of those closest to him since he felt sure they would recoil at the idea out of concern for his emotional health. In the first several weeks after the encounter, he never considered the notion. But since he had gotten a lot better yet still felt frustratingly fragile, he found himself pondering the possibility ever more.

He wanted to revisit the clearing in the woods. What was once unthinkable had gradually evolved into something not only doable, but desirable. Perhaps if he went back to the place of his greatest terror, it could no longer hurt him, or at least not as much. Had not those hospital doctors and that sweet lady psychiatrist all those years ago said he had to face his fears? Had they not warned how avoidance only intensified phobias all the more? Maybe, once he went back to the clearing, it would be so anticlimactic that he could kick himself for the rest of his life for foolishly waiting so long to return.

Or maybe he could suffer a relapse. Perhaps returning would be the worst possible thing he could do to trigger Lord knows what kind of hidden traumatic memories. No matter how often and for how long he kept weighing the potential pros and cons of going back, he could not decide what to do. But he had a gnawing sense he was going to return eventually. So why not now during a less stressful summer?

He would certainly not go alone. If General Longstreet would accompany him, that would be swell. Perhaps going with him would help bury any lingering unease his dog had about that awful night, though Elton had seen no evidence the general ever struggled with anything.

Who else should he ask to go with him? He could not imagine his brother or father wanting him to have anything to do with such an exercise, and he felt like a child asking either to join him. Plus, he would not want them to worry or be ticked off should he defy their advice, go back, and end up getting further psychologically scarred.

What about asking Otis Cummings or any of the other deputies who found him in the woods that night? They had been fascinated by that memorable night's events and enthusiastically plunged into *the UFO investigation* with far more eagerness than Sheriff Peabody. But he knew word would leak back to Bo. No deputy would dare take the sheriff's brother back to the clearing without first getting their boss's blessing. Besides, Elton would feel like a little boy asking a big deputy to protect him.

What about Kenley from the *Gazette*? She had become not only a friend but was a sister UFO buff whose excellent reporting made her quite possibly the county's leading authority on the whole matter. She was also a dream gal of a babe who he still hoped would one day become romantically unattached. Plus, he felt sure she would be ecstatic to not only go to the clearing but especially with the central player in its drama.

But what if he suffered some kind of terrible emotional reaction once there? What if they went into the woods and he got panicky and chickened out of finishing the journey? Even far worse, what if they got to the clearing and he started crying? Some picture of a strong man that would be. Just imagine what that might do to any hope of her ever dating him. Plus, even if they went to the clearing and the trek was successful, surely she would ask him to let her write a piece for the paper about it. He could easily hear her enthusiastic pitch for "Mr. Peabody returns to where the lights drama began." And he bristled at doing anything to revive waning local interest in the story or to prompt anyone to suspect he missed the limelight. Could such an article also prompt his family to ask just how shook up he had really been about the whole affair?

So who did that leave? With whom would he be comfortable on such an adventure and trust to neither be disappointed should he get scared, nor tell on him? It did not take long to realize the obvious choice.

Beryl McKenzie was not only his closest colleague, but the first friend he shared his entire encounter with and all the angst that came with it. Beryl had been totally supportive and understanding too. Furthermore, he was a fellow UFO buff whose entire life had been a very deliberate series of adventures. For once, Elton had an adventure eclipsing his friend's. There was no one with whom he felt more at ease daring to go back to that place. Indeed, he was confident Beryl would stand by him and never tell anyone anything he wanted hidden. And Elton would insist on going in the daytime. He could not see his friend saying no and, if the general joined them, what a terrific threesome they would be traversing the steps of his most consequential journey. He fondly recalled all the Oz novels he loved in which a colorful variety of human and animal characters would go on an exciting, suspenseful, but ultimately fun, satisfying, and safe journey, and often through the woods.

Mid-June marked the three-month mark since his encounter. *Time to man up*, Elton told himself. *Let's go back and try to put a period on this story. Even if it does not help, I will have the satisfaction of knowing I tried. I'm a lot better and stronger now and will increasingly feel like a coward if I don't.*

And he remembered the words of the Rev. Presseau. *Have faith*, he finally concluded. *Beryl and the general and I won't be alone.* That settled it.

CHAPTER 16

"Of course, I'll go with you," exclaimed Beryl. His face lit up the instant Elton asked. "I've been waiting three months for you to ask. I sure hoped you would anyway."

Beryl was so fired up about their excursion into the woods that they decided to do it next Saturday. Beryl could do it any day because he wrote and traveled on his own time each summer. Since his early summer had been consumed by writing short stories and starting his first novel, he was keen to get out of the house to spur some real-world excitement and hopefully create ideas for future stories. Elton even wondered if his friend had considered writing a fictional version of what he had gone through. If he did, he felt confident Beryl would do him right.

When "The Return," as Beryl jokingly dubbed their big day, arrived, they first met for an early lunch at Thai One On. Elton savored not only the superb food but how much more relaxed he was sharing a meal with his dearest friend than the last time he dined there with Kimberly, despite slightly dreading his and Beryl's post-meal destination. But he was struck by the lack of butterflies in his stomach.

Beryl deliberately kept matters light. In the days building up to "R-Day," as he laughingly told Elton, he had even debated what to wear on "the UFO hunt." For a hat, he finally settled on a fedora out of a 1940s film noir, something Humphrey Bogart would have worn as Detective Philip Marlowe in *The Maltese Falcon*. Beryl's hat topped his favorite tie-dyed, most psychedelic hippie shirt, a pair of well-worn blue jeans, and red sneakers. For dramatic flair, he considered taking a loaded pistol but vetoed the idea out of concern it could destroy the light mood. Instead, he packed his best camera.

The afternoon's purpose was not even mentioned during lunch. Instead they discussed a potpourri of mutual interests. Elton was relieved to have at least one friend with whom he never had to carry the conversation. Beryl could be a speed-rapper when excited, and Elton was the one friend he could never bore or exhaust with his long-winded, spontaneous verbal explorations of whatever he had recently read, heard, or seen. That they shared more common interests than with anyone else they knew—and could be completely candid with each other about anything—had long sealed their close friendship.

When through eating, they continued talking. Beryl did not want to rush his friend. Finally, Elton smiled and dramatically announced, "It is time for…'The Return.'"

"Operation R-Day begins!" Beryl laughed with relief.

They drove to Elton's house where General Longstreet was happy to welcome an old friend not seen in a while. He adored Beryl as one of Elton's friends who always greeted him with enthusiasm. The dog was doubly delighted when they all went in the backyard. Since it was rare for Elton to play fetch with him at 12:30 p.m., the general was extra pumped because he could sense something special was up. When Elton reached for the leash, Longstreet commenced dancing in circles, standing still just long enough to be leashed. Then they set out for the woods behind the backyard fence under an overwhelmingly blue, bright, hot sky.

"Weeee'reeee off to see the wizard," Elton started to sing, causing Beryl to chuckle with increasing confidence his friend would not turn back. Both focused on Longstreet, watching closely for any hint he might remember that March night and refrain from going into the woods. If he did, Elton dreaded the possibility the general might try to prevent him and Beryl from making the journey.

But Longstreet appeared more eager than they were to venture into the forest. He had only been in these woods once before and rarely got to go into any woods. So he was jumping at the leash. Could something subconscious be pulling his dog toward the forest all the faster? Elton speculated. *No, don't think like we're in the movies,* he told himself. *Just take one step at a time and focus completely on everything right here and right now.*

At last they got behind the fence and walked the last several feet of open grass to enter the woods. Elton was grateful for Beryl's constant chatter to help him zero in on the task at hand. Beryl had made him promise to speak up at the first signs of feeling panicky so they would immediately turn around. Elton was most appreciative but tried to assure him he felt better and better about this.

Unlike the lunch conversation, this one was consumed with UFO experiences they had read up on and seen documentaries about. Every few minutes Beryl asked if he was feeling okay. Soon he asked his friend to describe his original experience again. To his surprise, Elton did not feel his stomach muscles tighten or any other signs of fear. He found talking about what he saw, heard, and felt that night made this afternoon's experience less weird and frightening. General Longstreet seemed completely content to go at the leisurely pace they set, no longer pulling at the leash. And Elton was pleased to not hear any of his barking, growling, whining, or any other noises made that night in March.

Since there were no trails and the forest was thick as ever with trees and bushes, the walk was fairly slow. As hot and humid as it was outside the forest in mid-June, they enjoyed how much cooler it felt among the now-leafy trees. Unlike their absence the previous time he walked this way, Elton was relieved to hear the cheerful sounds of chirping birds and not the frenzied hoots from owls heard the last time he was here. He took comfort in sharing such observations with Beryl who was completely absorbed in the moment. To get to the right clearing, all Elton knew to do was just try to march in as straight a line as he could. Though he had noted a few such openings years before on his first trip through the forest, he was sure he would recognize the right one by everything being flattened.

After walking for what felt like too long not to have found the spot, Elton wondered aloud if they had gone past it. But they could see no openings among the trees in any direction. Maybe they should let the general guide them. But Elton would never forgive himself if he let Longstreet run and the dog ended up running away for good. So they patiently continued going forward, with Elton ever more relieved neither he nor Longstreet evinced any signs of panic. The whole walk seemed strange only because it felt so utterly normal and uneventful, with nary a hint of anything untoward ahead. Even if they were lost, Elton took comfort it was not even one in the afternoon and would not get dark this time of year until nine.

Suddenly, the general barked and jumped at the leash. Beryl and Elton had been so engrossed in conversation while navigating shrubs, fallen trees, and branches that they had not looked ahead in a while. At the general's bark, they immediately raised their heads to see what appeared to be a possible opening among the trees ahead. The bark had startled both of them, causing Beryl to laugh loudly. He had surprised himself, only now realizing how wound up he too had been. Though genuine, he deliberately amplified his laugh to reassure his friend.

Although jumping at his dog's bark, Elton quickly calmed down once he looked ahead to see nothing was wrong and the clearing could be within sight. Now peering forward with greater anticipation, the conversation stopped for the first time that day. General Longstreet appeared to be getting more excited but not angry or frightened. He only barked occasionally and as if he was just happy and eager to see or do something. As they continued walking, it became apparent there was in fact a clearing ahead, exactly in the direction where Elton remembered it.

So here it goes, he thought. *We're almost there and I'm still not feeling any fear: no butterflies in the stomach, goose bumps, shakes, or the urge to urinate.* Not one telltale sign of fear was upon him. In fact, he was excited to soon be where his life had changed three months before.

Ironically, the clearing was once again bathed in light, albeit this time from the sun. Just before they got to the edge of the opening, Longstreet got on his hind legs and began barking continuously. Confident he just wanted to seize the chance to race around the open area, Elton dropped the leash and the dog leaped into the clearing to do just that, again and again.

Before reaching the opening, Beryl turned to his friend and grinned. Elton looked back and caught himself smiling as well. What he had long thought of as a totally serious undertaking was turning out to be far lighter than imagined.

"Okay, buddy. This is it. Do we dare, Elton?"

"Absolutely."

As they walked into the clearing, Elton immediately declared, "This is it. Right here. We have arrived."

"The eagle has landed!" Beryl laughed, recalling the initial words spoken by the first astronaut to step onto the moon in 1969. Elton found himself quietly beaming as he slowly surveyed the entire little vista.

The area remained unusually flattened from that March night, which now seemed so long ago. The seedlings that had been pushed to the ground were growing again, just at a fairly pronounced angle. But there was a great deal of summer grass and many young bushes rising. Elton could find none of the yellowish sand the deputies collected that night, and the only burn marks were those of the remains of a campfire. The biggest change in the place's appearance were all the blatant signs of recent visitors—not little green aliens, but people. There were many beer bottles and cans strewn all over, especially around the campfire setting. There were so many, in fact, Elton wished they had brought a large trash bag so they could recycle them and clean up the otherwise scenic spot.

Suddenly Beryl began chortling at the big, spray-painted messages all over the ground: "Hello, Earthlings," "For a fun intergalactic time, call 1-800-big-star," "UFO Landing Site," and "Please Come Back!" Elton chuckled as well, rejoicing as waves of relief, irony, and humor washed over him. He and Beryl each wandered all over the roughly hundred-square-yard site to carefully examine everything. Meanwhile General Longstreet alternated racing around the clearing with sniffing each bottle, can, and anything else of interest. And marking his newfound territory.

"So, Mr. Peabody, what's it like being back at the scene of the most thrilling, frightening, mysterious night of your life?"

"Actually, my first date was nowhere near here," Elton quipped. Both laughed loudly at how wonderfully anti-climactic the experience had become. Fear was blessedly nowhere on anyone's radar screen.

"It's obvious this has become Johnston County's new top alternative tourist attraction," Beryl observed. "Heck, how many of our students—especially Mr. Peabody's—have made a pilgrimage right here to try to recreate their history teacher's mysterious encounter? I'm sure they came here at night too. That would explain the campfire. Who knows, buddy? One day this may be marked on maps as 'Cleburne's UFO landing site.'"

Elton had grown quiet. No longer tense or worried, he now felt comfortable trying to process all he had seen this afternoon.

"Everything still all right, buddy?"

"Oh, yes. I'm fine, thanks. I'm just trying to absorb both the banality and absurdity of it all. Rationally, I didn't expect us to find anything unusual, but I still had a sense anything could happen and a real hope that maybe, somehow, some answers could at last be found. Instead, the place is totally ordinary except for the campfire site, beer, and painted messages. It looks all so ridiculous now and, I guess, predictable. And I sure don't think we're going to find answers to any of the questions nagging me the last three months. But at least I manned up and faced my fears—some of them—with your help and the general."

Beryl winked and grinned. "I couldn't have returned here by myself either, man. Who could? Nobody honest."

"What happened to me here now seems like some kind of bizarre *Twilight Zone* version of this place, like a weird, inverted nightmare take on it. I feel like I have when visiting historic spots where some figure of history did something important right there, but now you'd never know it because it's in the middle of a busy street that thousands of people drive and cross every day, like where the Boston Massacre took place. I feel like I'm now in the satirical version of my encounter, the skit on *Saturday Night Live*. It's just surreal, man. If nothing else, hopefully this will help me not be as afraid. Shoot, I've been scared to even think about what happened."

"Relish this, buddy," Beryl urged him. "Think how much worse this could have been. What if we did see evidence of something from outer space or just really strange and scary stuff like in *The Blair Witch Project* film? How frightening, confusing, and frustrating would that be? Or imagine if there was nothing at all unusual here. How banal and boring would that be? And maybe you might even start to wonder if you had dreamed the whole thing up.

"But look at this. All this beer and these goofy messages prove people understand something super strange *did* happen here, really weird. Heck, half the Sheriff's Department followed a big light here and took all kinds of pictures and other evidence of some pretty funky doings that went down right here. So folks want to see this place. It's now special. And Elton Peabody helped put this little clearing on the map!"

Elton listened and smiled. What a relief to get another perspective on the topic he was most sick of mining on his own for what felt like so long.

"No place can project significance just by itself, unless it's uniquely beautiful," Beryl mused. "Nobody would notice the home where Martin Luther King Jr. grew up in Atlanta if there wasn't a historical marker in front of it. We have to give a place significance. It's a state of mind, man. Our whole world runs exactly all the way from our right ear…to our left ear."

"You're right, Beryl. And I appreciate all the insights. And yes, this was a good, even wonderful, and surefire memorable experience, and I thank you again so much for sharing it with me. I still wish it could give me some answers or even one sign. But so much of life remains a mystery."

Before they left, Beryl insisted on getting pictures of Elton with General Longstreet in front of the large "UFO Landing Site" message. Then they got a picture of all three of them before walking back.

While his friend resumed his speed rap, Elton quietly drifted ever further into his own world of wonder at how strange life could be: alternately mysterious, exciting, terrifying, troubling, mundane, and absolutely absurd. Was it really just a circus of different acts, "full of sound and fury and signifying nothing," as Shakespeare wrote? *Maybe,* he mused, *the best result of today's adventure is to just finally realize precious little makes sense in this thoroughly weird world. So we should stop worrying, set our speed at cruise control, and sit back to enjoy the ride.* How he regretted having fretted over so many fears throughout his life that proved to be utterly unfounded or trivial. *Wasting so much precious time worrying should have been my biggest fear,* he decided. *I don't know if today answered any big questions,* he concluded, *but at least I feel better for having finally made it happen. There's nowhere I'm afraid to go now,* he repeated to himself. And the "Please Come Back!" message was an especially fine touch.

CHAPTER 17

After his surprisingly satisfying return to the site of the incident, Elton did feel better about his entire ordeal. Enhanced all the more by the many humorous items found there, it was if a large period had finally descended, marking the end of the drama, at least regarding his fear that somehow the story was not yet over. For that he was genuinely relieved.

He would also be eternally grateful to Beryl and General Longstreet for accompanying him on what he hoped would be the closest adventure he would ever have to a spirit quest of some kind. It made him appreciate the value of true friendship more than ever and resolve to stand by any friend who reached out to him in need.

Aided by the sense he had at last completed some kind of circle—and one spiced with a deliciously funny and ironic twist at the end—for the first time he could imagine one day even writing about the affair. One day, but no time soon. He was still unsettled enough to deliberately stay busy and focus on many other things.

While attributing some of the remaining unease to lasting repercussions from the shock and terror he had experienced, he still wished for answers to satisfy him emotionally and intellectually. Though speaking with the Rev. Presseau and going back to the site did not provide definitive answers, he resigned himself to never being able to achieve that type of closure.

But each experience was deeply rewarding and helped further persuade him it would be okay if he never found out what truly happened. He tried convincing himself he was being unduly selfish to persist yearning so fervently for such clarity when everyone endured all kinds of unanswered questions and troubling mysteries. He also reminded himself how, unlike so many others, his involved no physical harm. And at the four-month anniversary, he was grateful for being in far better emotional shape than he had been.

Another summer school session was wrapping up well and ever fewer people were asking about his encounter. Sometimes he could go a whole week with no one inquiring what he thought he really saw on that now blessedly long ago night. Only a handful of his summer students had broached the subject with him and always alone after class. As was almost always the case with everyone asking, they were genuinely curious and sympathetic.

Elton's family grew increasingly relieved at how well their most sensitive child or sibling had handled himself. Sure, it had been a challenge and they could see how scared and unsure he had been at first, but they were delighted he appeared to be so much stronger than a dozen years before.

Yet they, Elton, and all who knew him well could tell he was not quite as talkative as he had been. They noticed him quietly looking down or just off in the distance more than before. His humor was not as present, and even the less cynical ones missed his occasionally acerbic wit.

It was with dread that Elton approached the end of summer classes in late-July. Now he would have his first few weeks with no work since Christmas holidays. While most folks relished such free time, he worried how to fill it to stay too busy to fall back into a deep funk. So he often traveled in early August and more than once with Beryl. They liked going to historic cities boasting sites associated with their favorite writers, historical figures, and events. But Beryl was working at a blistering rate, trying to finish what he hoped would be a completed initial draft of his first novel before being hit with five classes in mid-August. Elton's parents were tied up too.

So he did what he ideally did not like to do. He traveled alone. The irony was, once he got to a new city, he lost himself exploring it. He loved tracking down which president stayed where, walking through the historic district and downtown in general to absorb the ambiance of the place, savoring a variety of ethnic restaurants, and taking many pictures to share with students the next time he lectured on anything in that city. He also enjoyed the freedom to go wherever whenever, though it was a further irony his days on the road were tightly scripted with walking tours in the cooler mornings, museums in the hot afternoons, and ghost tours at night, with restaurants in between. For a change, it was also sweet to not be recognized as he inevitably was in Cleburne. Though he loved when former students said hello and how much they enjoyed his class, traveling afforded him the freedom to relax more. Out of town, he did not feel the need to always be "on," as he put it. This year's big summer trip would be all the more cherished for not having to answer questions about the night he still most wanted to forget.

Elton finally decided to go to San Francisco for his annual summer vacation. He had long heard about how beautiful it was, and he looked forward to exploring many historic sites. So he flew out west in early August and stayed at a charming old French hotel in the Nob Hill neighborhood that resembled a bed and breakfast, Le Petite Auberge. The staff was eternally friendly and helpful, he was grateful for the delicious and daily croissants, and he loved how early twentieth century European his room looked—replete with a fireplace—albeit with almost all modern amenities. Also splendid was the hotel's location within easy walking distance of most anywhere downtown, at least for someone with Mr. Peabody's energy and willingness to walk fast and far, and up and down those steep San Francisco hills.

So he had a big time going all over the city. But first, he was thrilled to take the boat out to Alcatraz Island to examine the famous prison, being careful to photograph 1920s' gangster Al Capone's cell. It surprised him how many varieties of lovely flowers graced the entire isle, and he reflected on how lonely it must have been for the prisoners to gaze longingly out of their cell-barred windows to see how vibrant, beautiful, and free the colorful city across the bay was while they were ensconced in drab, uniform, closed cells.

The highlight of Fisherman's Wharf was the USS *Pampanito* submarine from World War II. He was mesmerized walking through the cramped vessel, as he always was exploring warships but especially subs. He marveled at the remarkable bravery, discipline, and lack of claustrophobia the sailors aboard had to exhibit. Whenever he inspected such ships and places of battle, he inevitably wondered if he could have withstood the pressures of combat.

In a scrumptious contrast, the most magnificent hot chocolate he ever tasted was adoringly absorbed at the nearby Ghirardelli Square where the original chocolate factory once stood. Warm memories of the *Willy Wonka and the Chocolate Factory* movie infused him.

His favorite hotels to walk through were the famed old landmarks: the Fairmont, the St. Francis, and the Palace. In the last he tried to find the room where President Warren Harding died in 1921, but the room numbers had changed.

Chinatown was a hoot, and he smiled at the groups of Chinese playing Mahjong in the public square. Plus, the Chinese restaurant where he ate nearby was light years better than Cleburne's "Chinese" eatery. Proof of the former's authenticity was its lack of desserts or fortune cookies.

As usual on his travels, his best dining experience of all was Indian. Elton had long loved the subcontinent's cuisine better than any other, and he so wished one happy day an Indian eatery would grace Cleburne. The rich curries, tender meats, splendid spices, superb naan bread, rice pudding, and so many other varieties of food were all delightfully delicious. Even vegetables he normally abhorred, like cauliflower, carrots, and squash, somehow tasted marvelous when rendered Indian-style. The food was also the most colorful he had ever seen. How he liked to just look at the jet-red Tandoori chicken. And to drink a mango lassi was liquid heaven.

At this particular Hindu haunt, he had a most memorable experience when drying his hands in the men's room. An old Indian gentleman was heading to the sink and smiled at him. Suddenly he straightened up and raised his index finger to make a pronouncement.

"De tree most important tings in life: religion, food, toilet."

"Amen." Elton smiled. He told himself he would have to share this with Beryl.

On the sightseeing front, the wannabe writer in him lit up when he spied City Lights Bookstore and the bar next door where Dylan Thomas, Jack Kerouac, and Allen Ginsberg could each be found perhaps writing and definitely drinking long ago. Elton called Beryl to give him a live take on the North Beach site he knew his poet buddy would most appreciate.

The area of town giving Mr. Peabody the most pleasure was the old hippie district of Haight-Ashbury. That was the source of so much of his favorite music from the late 1960s and early 1970s. So he was elated to play detective and track down the various former abodes of Jimi Hendrix, Janis Joplin, Big Brother and the Holding Company, the Grateful Dead, and the Jefferson Airplane. The spectacularly detailed Victorian architecture of the neighborhood was everywhere enhanced by a kaleidoscope of colors. And nearby Golden Gate Park was a sparkling jewel of greenery and flowers.

But the most fun of all in San Francisco was riding the cable cars. How he felt like a boy on a roller coaster again standing on the side of each car holding onto the bar tightly as the vehicle raced downhill with the brisk wind slapping his face. Each time he caught himself grinning.

He put together two photo albums from the trip, being careful to write in their margins as many details as possible about each historic site to hopefully excite the students when passed around class. In addition to piquing their interest in whatever San Francisco-related topic was being discussed, he hoped to inspire students to try to travel, knowing many had never been out of state.

It was not only a happy trip, but all the more satisfying for his having been alone for a full week for the first time he could recall, and he had not succumbed to any extended bouts of anxiety or depressive funks concerning the encounter. Yes, he had made sure to create jam-packed itineraries each day to keep him preoccupied, but he always did that anyway.

So when he reached the five-month anniversary of the start of the rest of his life, as he now conceived it, he gratefully acknowledged that, though some anxiety remained, he was getting close to feeling normal again, at least for him. And, though not enthused about all the grading which would soon ensue or encounters with the likes of educrats like Mr. Sneed, Elton looked forward to teaching again with the return of fall classes in mid- to late-August. He also wondered if he should dare hope to not be asked a single question about his encounter. How sweet it would be to not have to recall that night again except by his own choice. Heck, if no one asks anymore, maybe he would even miss the attention. Maybe not, he mused.

18

CHAPTER

On the Sunday before fall classes began, Elton was at the First Presbyterian Church. His Sunday school class led by Dr. Isaac "Slim" Patterson, a professor at the local Stonewall Jackson Community College, had been thought-provoking, as it almost always was. Elton appreciated how the old gentleman would begin each class with a prayer, read a story from the Bible, explain what he thought was the real message of the Scriptures shared, and then segue into posing questions for the class to discuss. At one point during that morning's discussion, it suddenly hit Elton how no one in the class had asked about his March encounter in months. Nor had any brother or sister parishioners treated him any differently than usual. With gratitude, he relished how life appeared to be returning to the refreshingly routine.

Afterward he enjoyed seeing his entire family sitting together in the pulpit for the 11:00 worship service. It was a special smiler his sister Melody was visiting. As he sat in the pew, he noted nothing unusual about the prayers, hymns, announcements, or sermon that day, but Elton reflected on how comforting the rhythms of the service had become to him. Following the service, in the receiving line to greet the Rev. Presseau, he suddenly decided to thank his pastor again for having talked with him at length about his encounter and to tell him how very much better he was now. The minister beamed.

"It's always swell to visit with you, Elton. God has been good to you. Very good. And you have worked hard, Elton. I'm so proud of you, son, and thank you for the joyful update."

Then the Peabody family enjoyed its weekly Sunday lunch at the old home place. It was extra sweet that Melody could join them. She was the favorite aunt for Bo and Stevie's young daughters, Sarah and Esther. They treasured how she was their one aunt who would always play with them, and enthusiastically too.

After the meal, the adults remained at the table to leisurely update each other about their previous week. The family patriarch, Joshua, recounted how well the farm was doing, and Ruth and Melody told of their looking forward to classes starting back that week. Bo recounted how very much better his reelection-free summer had gone than the winter or spring, and Stevie conveyed how sad but excited she was that six-year-old Sarah would be starting first grade.

When it was Elton's turn to share what he had been up to since they last met, he hesitated. Usually when asked by anyone but Beryl how he was doing, he would simply speak in broad generalities to avoid mentioning whatever was stressing him. But he had been in a pensive mood at church that morning and was increasingly accepting the notion he was now mostly over his encounter from over five months before, and surely the worst of it. The topic had never been raised in the presence of the entire family, but Elton thought his closest kin would appreciate what he wanted to say.

"I'm looking forward to classes too," he began slowly. "But there's not really much news on that front. However, I can say that, just over five months after my big UFO encounter last March, I no longer feel like it's always on my shoulder. It's ever further in my rearview mirror, and I'm increasingly okay with not knowing what happened."

As soon as he mentioned his encounter, no one moved, and all eyes were on him. Indeed, no one could recall when the family's first-born had ever brought up a painful personal struggle at the dinner table, but all were enormously relieved to hear how well he was doing. While everyone else sat expressionless, Elton's mother began to beam.

"And I want to thank y'all so very, very much," he continued, "for all your invaluable help during this whole saga. Y'all have been extra considerate, patient, kind, and supportive…and loving. And I know I'm now in a whole lot better place than I was, and it's in no small measure due to y'all. So I want y'all to know how big a help you've been and there's no need to worry about me any more…at least not about UFOs." He chuckled. "Endless thanks."

Bo patted his brother on the back, but let their father speak first. Joshua Peabody was nodding his head slowly.

"Son, you've come a mighty far piece in this whole matter, and your mother and I couldn't be prouder of you, boy."

"Same here," Bo and Stevie quickly added while Melody eagerly nodded and grinned.

"You're a whole lot stronger than you think you are, Elton," his mother told him.

"It's been an adventure for all of us," Bo said. "Lord knows, 'the Friday night lights' has been the top topic of conversation at the Sheriff's Department this year. And shoot, it is a whole heck of a lot more fun to talk about than burglaries, gangs, drugs, or most of the rest of the stuff we have to deal with. Why don't you have another UFO experience, brother?" He winked.

As they laughed, each rejoiced, knowing the family had successfully weathered a major storm and emerged not only united but stronger. Elton, in particular, felt this would be a moment he would not forget.

Later that afternoon, Mr. Peabody had an encounter of a very different kind while walking in downtown Cleburne by the statue of Confederate General Joe Johnston, the county's namesake. He was lost in thought when he heard someone slowly drawl, "Well, hello, Mr. Peabody." Before she finished her sentence, he knew who it was.

"Well, how goes it, Miss Penelope?" He smiled. His former student gave him a hug and a kiss on the cheek before asking how his summer had gone. She particularly enjoyed his amusing tale about what he found returning to the UFO site with her old English teacher.

"Oh, that gives me an idea!" she gushed. "Let's you and me go back to that site, but at night during the UFO witching hour. You can flag down another UFO, but this time we'll go aboard and up into outer space together. Then just think. You and I will be Earth's first interstellar couple. Tres cool."

"Have you been smoking any 'herbal jazz cigarettes,' as Sir Paul McCartney called them?"

"No, sir. Just dreaming of you. Fantasizing, if truth be told." She giggled.

"You never stop, do you?"

"Not when sexy Mr. Peabody's the topic," she barely got out before doubling over in laughter.

"Enough." Elton shook his head, trying valiantly not to laugh.

She had worked as a lifeguard at the beach since her father owned some property there. It was the same job she had enjoyed the last two summers.

"There were some real cute college boys there." She sighed. "But I told them all I'm still saving myself for you, Mr. Peabody... Elton, now that I'm graduated." She grinned. "Just like you've been saving yourself for me all these years, right, Elt?" She laughed.

"Great. I'm sure there's now much wailing and gnashing of teeth among cute college boys everywhere," Mr. Peabody deadpanned, prompting Penelope to almost fall into Gen. Johnston laughing.

"So have you thought of me any?" she asked.

"Actually, I have," he replied truthfully, causing her face to light up.

"Fantasizing about me, huh?"

"Oh, yeah. Every day." He rolled his eyes, prompting more chuckles.

"Then how have you thought of me?" she inquired. "I'm serious."

He looked in her eyes and paused. Miss Breen's eyes suddenly widened, and she began to grin.

"Well, Miss Penelope, the gospel truth is that you were actually quite a hoot to teach. You paid close attention to the lectures and thought about them enough to pose really provocative questions no one else would ask. You made me think through and explore different sides of historical actors. You sometimes—*sometimes*—made some super sharp observations and got us all to examine some things we likely wouldn't have considered otherwise. And you were occasionally pretty witty. I tried not to laugh in class, but afterward I often smiled about something you said.

"I've just never had a student as willing to challenge the conventional party line as you. You displayed a certain fearlessness I envy. Indeed, you dared to pose questions I didn't have the guts to ask in class and thus gave me a chance—the excuse—to explore some fascinating angles of events and people I wouldn't have but for you. And I can't think of any other student who's done that remotely as much as you. So yes, you have been a special student who I expect to miss, especially once classes start up again."

"Oh, now you're going to make me cry," she said softly and gave him a hug. For the first time in all four years of knowing her, the everbrash, slyly grinning, mischievous Miss Breen suddenly appeared like a shy girl close to tears.

"Oh my goodness, could the legendary Penelope Breen actually be *at a loss for words?*"

"Maybe. Just for a minute anyway. But thank you, Mr. Peabody. That was the nicest thing any teacher has ever told me. Or maybe any adult. By far."

"Never forget how smart and capable you are, Penelope. I know you can turn guys' heads and be socially commanding, but it's your brains that can take you just about wherever you want. So make sure you use them to earn whatever degree or degrees that excite you the most. I know there'll be a slew of cute college boys, but don't major in men. Have some fun, but please never forget your schooling will determine the direction of your life. So don't get too distracted."

"Wow. You really do care about me, Mr. Peabody. Thank you." She smiled and patted his shoulder. "But you're still Elton to me from now on or just Elt." She winked.

"And I hope you'll let me know how you're doing, Miss Penelope. I'd like to see how the legendary Miss Breen grows up. I wouldn't be shocked to see you as a movie star, a novelist, or an astronaut…or a wonderful wife and mother, or all of them. Thank you for adding a delightful dose of color to an all-too-often black-and-white world."

"I may be president too."

"I can see that as well. I would not be stunned. And oh, the stories I can tell." He smiled.

"You could be my First Gentleman."

"Let's focus on college first, dear. Best wishes always."

They exchanged contact information, hugged, and said good-bye. While it was a thrill to visit with graduated students he had enjoyed having in class, such experiences had a poignant quality too. Yes, he felt blessed to interact with so many interesting personalities and really kind folks in his classes, and it was a genuine joy to get to know and hopefully help awaken them to new areas of interest and possibilities. Yet they would all too soon leave and be gone forever. The last week of school each May was especially bittersweet because each class had been a little community of students with its own unique collective personality that would soon disappear and never regroup. *Just be grateful and enjoy each ride,* he tried to reassure himself.

The new school year started and was nothing extraordinary. The week before classes began saw the faculty having to sit through the same annual bat squat nonsense from professional educrats droning on and on about the latest fads plaguing the ever-expanding, vast educational-industrial complex, and all the new paperwork teachers needed to address. As usual, Mr. Peabody sat in the back with Beryl and Luke Frazier, his favorite colleagues, whispering snide remarks about each speaker, gossiping, reading, and writing. Elton wished he had taken a good class on how to meditate even in the worst settings. A game the three liked to play was penning poems together with Beryl writing a verse, then Luke, and then Elton. Each poem would satirize the various educrats speaking, as well as teachers not on their Christmas card list. Each writer tried to break up the others, inevitably causing them all to crack up. Elton shuddered at how lonely and bored to anger he would be at these endless meetings without fun friends. And he resented all the many hours of his life needlessly sacrificed on the altar of educrats' egos.

The next week his new classes were amusingly lively yet thankfully shy of rambunctious. The students appreciated his dramatic lecture performances, especially his humor. Many who had not taken him before were glad to finally have a teacher who commanded their attention by putting on a show. They also liked how he tried to be fair to every historical figure or group, arguing both sides or exploring a range of opinions on each. Mr. Peabody recoiled at bitter memories of so many of his high school, college, and graduate school instructors who preferred to indoctrinate instead of teach. It struck him as especially ironic that so many of the teachers who most loudly preached *diversity, multiculturalism, inclusion,* and *tolerance* exhibited the least tolerance for any diversity of ideas, opinions, philosophies, religious perspectives, or political parties other than their own. Mr. Peabody saw all attempts to pressure students into adopting whatever was the prevailing politically correct party line or any other perspective as an abuse of the instructor's authority. Besides, he had changed his mind on so many matters in his thirty-five years that he lacked the confidence to try to impose any view on anyone, much less impressionable teenagers.

The resumption of classes each fall reminded him of just how very blessed he was to have so many hopeful students eager to learn and still open to fresh ideas. Many continued to have such a sweet, "Disneyfied" view of life which he wondered how long they could retain. He had to have meaning in his life to get out of bed each day and, despite all life's troubles, his job enabled him to believe he was making a tangibly positive difference in many people's lives. How sad to see so many colleagues—many younger than himself—already beaten down and not really interested in their jobs. He wondered when and why they lost their mojo to teach and whether they had ever enjoyed the job. Indeed, he saw so many people in general who did not show much passion for anything. *How wonderful it would be,* he thought, *if we could figure out how our students could hold onto their sense of wonder and excitement about the world throughout the inexorable struggles of life.* How he hoped he would always look forward to his lectures, club meetings, and general interactions with students.

On the immediate front, it was a super swell smiler only a few new students that week asked about his UFO encounter and always respectfully after class. He no longer dreaded the question and could even enjoy speculating about what may have really happened. He was intrigued by their various opinions and more than once had to bite his lip to keep from laughing when a student sincerely came up with a particularly original explanation.

"Mr. Peabody, do you think they could have been an advanced guard of Satan's Air Force?" remained his favorite student theory.

"I'd have to think about that," he answered. "But that's certainly an intriguing concept."

Now he would add the story of his return to the site with Mr. McKenzie and General Longstreet and the funny spray-painted messages found—though he edited out the beer bottles and cans. A couple of students volunteered how they heard of folks going there after all the news stories about *the clearing in the woods*. Elton relished how the event appeared to be ever more relegated to the past, especially among students whose lives were so fixated on the present.

The sole sour experience he had about his encounter that first week of classes came from a predictable source: Assistant Principal Frank Sneed. As Elton was walking down the hall, he had been unable to avoid the school's disciplinarian walking toward him. As Elton gave him a polite smile—he still could not deign to speak to the man—Mr. Sneed asked as he walked past him,

"Seen any more little green men, Elton?"

Initially stunned but quickly acknowledging he should have expected such, Elton decided to turn around and retort in the same spirit.

"Only you, Frank."

For a split second, he thought he detected the slightest stumble in Mr. Sneed's normally quick stride. When no reply came, Elton turned around and, noticing the reflection in his classroom window, saw Mr. Peabody was sporting a wide grin.

After the first week of the new academic year, he believed he had cleared yet another hurdle and the March encounter had shrunk into a significantly smaller image in his rearview mirror. Yes, it still gave him many moments of anxiety and all the original questions remained, but there was so much less urgency to them now and ever more confidence he would somehow stumble through, as he eventually had with every other problem. It struck him how one of the advantages of approaching middle age was the growing sense that, whatever awful struggles life threw at you, you could probably think of others you had somehow gotten through before that were even worse. His biography had also taught him even a failure or crisis could open opportunities and lead one to a better place than one's previous path might have afforded. He did not dare yet hope that would prove to be the case with his encounter, but nor did he rule out the possibility anymore.

CHAPTER 19

Mr. Peabody was leaving work on the second day of classes in the new school year. It had been another good day of lectures and trying to learn the new students' names and personalities. As he walked down the hall, he mulled over the pros and cons of each lecture, as well as how he could do better next time. It was a daily ritual to improve his teaching. He also made notes about which students he should pay close attention to for various reasons: any with possible emotional problems he should be extra protective toward, cut-ups he should rein in fast, those with a foul attitude who he would try to bring around, and the academically strongest and least shy ones to call on to start a discussion. He was lost in thought when suddenly a gorgeous young lady rounded the corner and came face-to-face with him.

She was a tall twenty-something whose beauty was so pronounced it was hard to look away. Draped by a mane of long, blond, curly hair was a face which reminded him of flawless-looking statues of Greek and Roman goddesses. Elton had noticed her in the previous week's faculty meetings but had not met her. She sat on the other side of the room with most of the English Department. Though, even at a distance, she stood out as mighty attractive, until now he had no idea just how hypnotically enchanting her Pacific blue eyes were. Despite her voluptuous figure outfitted in a bright red shirt, gold skirt, and black high heels, it was her enchanting eyes that seized his gaze. They were the bluest and clearest he had ever seen. He found himself wanting to dive into them to see if he could find any flaw. Nor had he come across such plump, pretty pink lips. They did not appear to have any lipstick, and their large size balanced those beautiful big, blue eyes.

"Hey there," she said with a beaming smile. He was slightly startled since his experience had been that he typically greeted folks first.

"Hello," he answered. "You must be one of our new teachers." She extended her hand and he noted how long her fingers were, sporting superbly manicured nails and a couple of large silver rings. One finger had an aqua-colored tattoo. Her hand appeared both elegant and bohemian. Though the hand felt soft, she gave him a much firmer grip than he was used to with ladies.

"Yes. Essielya McGahee. I'm your new English teacher."

"Elton Peabody. I teach history."

"I noticed you at the orientation meetings last week." She grinned.

He got what felt like a rush of endorphins since he could not remember when a pretty lady had ever said such to him. Should he reply that he—as well as Beryl and Luke—had certainly noticed her too? Or would that reflect badly on him for not introducing himself earlier to welcome her to the school? And why did she have such a mischievous grin mentioning she noticed him?

"You, Mr. McKenzie, and that other guy always sat in the very back and seemed in y'all's own world whispering to each other, laughing, and passing something around. And it looked like each of you would write on it too. I kept trying to figure out what y'all were doing."

"Ah, we were taking turns adding a verse to a poem…that typically made fun of whichever educrat was speaking," he slowly stated, careful to note whether her facial expression appeared to approve.

"Oh, I love it." She giggled. "Why couldn't I think of doing that? Of course, it might not be kosher for the new gal trying to make a good impression and sitting near her department chairman. But what a hoot. Good for you. Can I sit with y'all at faculty meetings from now on?"

"Sure. Do you like poetry?"

"I love poetry, reading and writing it."

"Wow. I've just met a real live poetess," Elton exclaimed. "Your brother English teacher, Beryl McKenzie, is a published poet."

"Oh, I know. And I like his poems too. He's such a dear—so witty, interesting, and enthusiastic as well. I can see why the students adore him. I hear they also love Mr. Peabody."

"I'm quite blessed. It's a joy to have a job where I get paid to think, read, write, and talk about what I think, read, write, and talk about on my own anyway. I'd do it for free but haven't told the principal."

"Don't you dare." She grinned.

"The students are so sweet too—most of them—and I love sharing history with them. I still get excited revealing information I've read in some new biography, and it's great how most are still open to new concepts."

"It's obvious you love teaching. Your face came alive just now talking about it." She smiled. "May I call you Elton?"

"Oh, yes. And, forgive me, how do you pronounce your name?"

"It's just like Cecilia, but replace the *Ce* with *Es*."

"Like the Simon and Garfunkel song 'Cecilia,'" Elton enthused.

"I love Simon and Garfunkel." Essielya beamed.

Miss McGahee had grown up in another little town in the state but had gone to college and then taught a few years in a big city. Elton thought that might explain how she effortlessly blended such a suave vibe with slightly earthy common sense. Though she had done quite well teaching at an urban school, she missed the rhythms of a small town and was thrilled to get the gig in Cleburne, which reminded her so much of her hometown.

The conversation veered into mutual musical and literary interests, and Elton found himself able to converse with Essielya more comfortably than with many folks he had known his whole life. Indeed, her complete candor liberated him to be more frank than he was with most. He also found himself feeling mesmerized by her eyes, as well as slightly narcotized by her femininely soft, soothing, Southern drawl. Her eyes never left his, and he was absorbed in the most enchanting aura of positivity and happiness which she seemed to emanate effortlessly. Normally he was easily distracted in conversation, especially in the school halls, by people walking by, whatever new flyers had been put on bulletin boards, and all the sounds accompanying so many adolescents. But not now. He knew he had never met anyone like this. No one in his life had projected such an easy-going attitude of kindness, friendliness, confidence without the least arrogance, and even a touch of playful mischief.

He was also taken with how many subjects they both adored and how genuinely interested she appeared to be in him and his opinions. Just as he mused how she must be a superb actress if she's not, she startled him by asking to see his classroom since she was curious to look at all his posters of American heroes and the historical artifacts he had just mentioned. No colleague had ever made that request, he noted.

Upon entering his work lair, Essielya let out an "Oh, look at this," as she slowly circled the room to carefully examine and ask about each item on display. Elton was charmed just looking at how her eyes sparkled and her whole face would shine recognizing various show-and-tell items.

"This is exactly what I'm trying to do with my classroom," she exclaimed. "I've put up posters of so many of my favorite novelists, short story writers, and poets. You should come see it."

"I'd love to," he replied. Never had such a remarkably attractive lass spontaneously given him so much attention, and he realized she was carrying most of the conversation too. He felt a pronounced sense of dreamy calm and tried to discern why. Then it occurred to him that he was not consciously performing or trying oh so hard to impress. *Just look at how much more relaxed I am,* he marveled.

But it was when she occasionally touched him with a soft pat on the shoulder or a quick touch of his arm while making a point that he felt his whole being tingle. After a while he detected a warmth centered in his chest that seemed to slowly engulf his whole body. He reveled in just looking at and listening to her. Though conveying such energy and engagement with everything around her, she still projected a pronounced sense of regal calm. For Elton, she could have been speaking Dutch since he was completely satisfied to just luxuriate in her presence and stay buzzed by her hypnotic voice. He could not recall when anyone had induced such a pleasantly hazy sense of well-being or even contentment in him. When they finished touring his classroom, she saw the clock on the wall and gasped slightly.

"Oh, I'm so sorry I've taken up over an hour of your time and so delayed your going home," she apologized.

"It could have been ten minutes for all I knew. This has been the highlight of my day," Elton answered truthfully.

"Mine too," she replied. "Next time I'll show you my room."

"Deal," he immediately declared. They continued talking while walking to the parking lot. Now Elton was answering questions about various educrats and the ways of the school. She was grateful for his insights, and he was glad to have another fellow educator who loved to teach and adored her students. It was always a splendid smiler when he and a new colleague appeared to be simpatico, but this felt like an entirely different level of connection.

After comparing notes about colleagues and students for another half hour under the hot August sun, they finally parted. Elton found himself walking slower to his car and did not think much driving home. Instead he turned off the radio to try to drown in the brilliant blue sea of tranquility engulfing him. There would be plenty of time to retrace everything she said and to analyze each facial expression. He had all night for that, he mused. When had he ever been stopped and captivated by such an enchanting, fascinating, and stunningly fetching presence? When had he ever beheld anyone who could emanate so many positive emotions?

When he played fetch with General Longstreet, he saw himself as a distant character in a film since his mind was in a place it rarely went, a kaleidoscope of pleasing thoughts without words. Though he ate dinner over an hour and a half later than usual, he felt no hunger pangs. Afterward he just lay on the sofa trying to replay what struck him as perhaps the most significant encounter he had had in over five months. The general noted his pensive mood and lay down by his side so Elton could rub his head.

He put on a Duke Ellington album and got lost in its majestic rhythms of mystery and joy. He was especially enchanted by the addictive chords of "On a Turquoise Cloud." The maestro's understated piano melody beautifully underscored the hypnotic, high-pitched soprano vocals of Kay Davis. Wordless yet engrossing, they struck him as the hypnotic sounds that a scintillating siren on a haunted island might project toward a passing ship at night in hopes of serenading it into her amorous embrace.

Elton had reached that special plane of contentment where thoughts are wordless and all images tranquil. Totally absorbed in the lovely sounds coming from the speakers, he was reminded of the first time he got stoned. That same drowsy, dreamy calm had utterly captured him again, and he relished the sense that all was well, wishing it could last. Then he recalled the paranoia each time he had gotten high and why he had never touched any recreational drugs since college. Reality returned and the song ended.

When the absent-minded, mildly drugged feeling finally left him, he found familiar old warnings invading his dreamscape. *Don't get infatuated with such a modelesque gal who would never go out with me. Maybe she's just using me for information about her new job and is a tad lonely in a new town. Besides, stunners like that always have a boyfriend or are married. Even if she miraculously dated me, what chance would I have it could last? I've had a whole heap of hurt these last five months and don't need heartbreak too, and how awful to have a romantic relationship at school go sour. That could poison the work environment for years. And stop kidding myself. Babes like her are just not interested in an average-looking, non-athletic professional nerd like me.* Reality now pounded furiously on his door.

But she had initiated every step in their getting-to-know-each-other and chose to spend all that time with him. Even if they never dated, he was confident he had at least made a new friend or, at a minimum, a friendly acquaintance or colleague. He could just enjoy her company when they saw each other at school and be appreciative of that.

Yet he knew he would try to ask her out. At thirty-five, his life had already endured way too many missed opportunities and he was not going to casually blow another. Even if she turned him down, they could remain friends and he would not have to live with bitter regret at never having tried to court her. Though several of her fingers were ringed, he saw no wedding band. So he resolved to take up the offer to visit her classroom and see if she was still full of *joie de vivre* and seemingly taken with him.

First, to either bolster his determination or forfeit the match, he called Beryl since he and Essielya were in the same department and had therefore had departmental meetings together the week before. He trusted Beryl's judgment more than anyone else at work.

"Oh, she's a sweetheart, all right," enthused his friend. "Quite a looker too. She knows her stuff and has a real positive attitude about teaching. I'm impressed with her."

"She and I had such a fine time talking literature and all kinds of topics today, and I just found her entrancing," Elton gushed.

"You should ask her out, man. How often, especially in a small town, do you get to meet someone that hot who shares so many interests and has such a kind persona too? And as my daddy told me, 'Only date a gal who, if she were a guy, would be your friend.' Is that not Miss Essielya?"

Mr. Elton's next day was a blur of classes and all the other tasks he set for himself: revising lesson plans, talking with students, checking e-mail, reading, paperwork, and a seemingly endless parade of more. But he sought to stay extra busy to avoid being distracted by the shining new presence on his horizon. It had always been a challenge to focus on and hopefully get consumed by the lectures since anxious thoughts rarely stopped banging on his door. Today he was more concerned about particularly pleasant ones.

When the last class wrapped, he worked extra fast to finish the day's work and prepare for tomorrow's classes to hopefully get to Essielya's classroom before she left. When he found her room, he was impressed to see Miss McGahee still working at her desk. As soon as he knocked, he was delighted to see her flash a big smile and jump up to greet him.

"Mr. Elton! How sweet of you to take up my invitation to see my classroom." After asking how he was doing, she proceeded to show all the many posters of her literary heroes and heroines lining the walls. Elton was elated to see most were his as well: Mark Twain, Emily Dickinson, L. Frank Baum, F. Scott Fitzgerald, Zora Neale Hurston, John Steinbeck, George Orwell, Flannery O'Connor, Harry Crews, Michael Faudet, and Lang Leav. They compared notes on their favorite books by each and then Elton asked how her first week of classes was panning out. She was very pleased with how "darling" her students were and how friendly and helpful so many of her colleagues appeared too. She even laughed about the few boys who had already hit on her.

"Oh, they were just being cute. But I set them straight about boundaries between teachers and students." She laughed. "Hopefully I didn't embarrass or hurt their feelings too much."

Like the day before, their conversational adventure leisurely meandered in a variety of directions. There were no pauses, and Elton found himself speaking more than yesterday and more excitedly. He treasured the return of that same dreamy sense of satisfaction but was more fully engaged in the discussion since he was able to focus better.

Essielya was quite enjoying herself with this new colleague. She could not recall the last time she found a young man who shared remotely her passion for literature, especially poetry. She was also flattered he appeared sincerely interested in her views. Indeed, he often asked her opinion and did not even interrupt when she gave it. He had a self-deprecating wit that was sometimes acerbic but never mean, and she was taken with his animated enthusiasm for many of her favorite topics. Furthermore, she appreciated how he maintained eye contact—exceedingly rare for a man of any age in her experience—and came across as a Southern gentleman.

Miss McGahee was finding her new town and job to be working out quite well indeed. It was refreshing to once again be in a community that was overtly friendly, polite, and less formal than the big city. She kept being reminded of her beloved hometown and was grateful for the slower pace. Very importantly, her new students, colleagues, and even the educrats were all shaping up to be positive too. The one downside was loneliness due to not really knowing anyone yet. But she had never had trouble making friends and was intrigued by and excited about this history teacher.

After almost an hour of increasingly fast-paced discussion on a dizzying slew of topics, Elton surprised himself and asked her out. Never had he done that in person. It had always occurred over the phone after being repeatedly rehearsed. But he just felt such a strong link between them that he decided to be somewhat impulsive. Even if she turned him down, he guessed it would be better to get it out of his system now and not be more disappointed later. So he asked if she would like him to take her to one of his favorite local eateries Friday. Normally he would propose seeing a film afterward as well, but he preferred just talking with her instead. *Exactly which film could ever be as captivating as this incredible chick?* he thought.

"I'd love to." She smiled. "We can continue our conversation at length. I want to quiz you about the town too, since you grew up here. Can you pick me up at six?"

"Will do, dudette." She gave him directions to her apartment, and they exchanged cell phone numbers. For the first time there was a pause in their conversation, but neither felt awkward. They just looked into the other's face and smiled.

For a brief moment while leaving work late that Wednesday, Elton Peabody wondered if he had been too hard in his assessment of this life. Suddenly everything appeared so much more as it should be with nothing to worry about. He realized he was in the midst of a new emotional high that could easily come collapsing down, but he was going to stretch it out as long as possible. Even if Essielya McGahee never went out with him again, even if she stood him up Friday, he had at least two whole days to be excited. Though typically a nervous, distracted neurotic on a first date, he was more sure of himself this time. Indeed, he was convinced he already knew this lady pretty well, a lot better than any other first date he could recall. And he was confident he had at least made a bona fide friend. How inspiring they made such easy and engrossing conversation, and she talked more than him. He did not even feel the need to perform. Elton just had a fine feeling about this Friday night, no matter his dating history.

CHAPTER 20

Thursday at work went all right for Elton. He was pleased with his lectures, and the first Presbyterian Club meeting of the year had gone exceedingly well with a whopping fifteen students attending. It was always a victory when club attendance hit double figures, particularly the first week of the school year. There were seven returning students and eight new ones. Mr. Peabody had gently plugged the club in his classes and was gratified to see several of his new students checking out the group. He was relieved last year's club president, Elasiah Edmonds, was back and confirmed her desire to run for president again. As the group's first black leader, he hoped she could continue to recruit more minority members. It was also a victory six boys showed up in the historically girl-dominated club.

Elton was growing more optimistic about the new school year. In fact, he could not remember one starting better. Of course, he knew the greatest source of excitement, and his cautious optimism about the next evening was enhanced when Beryl confided Essielya said she thoroughly enjoyed chatting with him. Elton was touched his dearest friend would share that and was glad his old buddy was her officially designated mentor.

That night Elton's mother called to ask how the new school year had begun. He was pleased to tell both parents how well things appeared to be going but did not dare mention Essielya. He had always carefully avoided apprising his parents about his dating life. Why risk their disapproval, especially since he was going to do what he wanted anyway? While it was unspoken, they each acknowledged how very much better he was doing than just a few months ago.

Mrs. Peabody told her son how much his older niece Sarah was already enjoying first grade. Though Stevie cried after dropping her off at school the first day, she had not done so since and was relieved her elder daughter was enjoying school. Ruth Peabody reiterated how much less stressful it was for everyone to have Bo's reelection campaign behind them. Yes, there was the general election in November, but the party primary in the spring was the one that counted since Bo did not even have an opponent in the fall. His sister Melody was also doing fine, happy to report her new school year had started well.

It was just after ten as Elton lay on the sofa to read when his phone rang. When he saw who was calling, his heart swelled. It was Essielya. Then the thought occurred perhaps she was phoning to cancel about tomorrow. *That would certainly be a return to reality,* his cynical side thought. *Ah, well, it's still been fun to dream for a while,* he reasoned. And at least she had the class to call a day early.

But she said she was bored and lonely and just wanted to chat. Elton was not only relieved but touched she would confess the new gal in town felt alone and wanted a friendly ear. Their conversation flowed as easily as before and, without the striking visual distraction, this time Elton could zero in on every word. The chat updated many previous topics before delving into more personal realms, like each one's upbringing and religious, cultural, and political views. To their delight, once again their paths repeatedly overlapped. Both grew up on a farm in a traditional Protestant family; he was Presbyterian and she was Baptist. Each had long struggled to accept all the dimensions of the family faith; however, they believed in God, the basic Judeo-Christian morals, and prayed daily. Each confided how, despite their difficulty accepting the veracity of many biblical stories, living with the mystery of the miracles and other supernatural phenomena was infinitely preferable to the terrible ache of believing this life was all there was and we were completely on our own. Both readily confessed needing God far too much to embrace anything but the religion in which they were reared. Elton invited her to visit First Presbyterian Church with him anytime, and she said she might well do that.

Essielya asked, "Isn't everything a mystery? I mean, what in life do we really know for certain? How can we? We're not God. As tough as it is sometimes to accept some of the Bible or tenets of the church on faith, don't we have to have faith to do anything?"

"Right. Shoot, we have to have faith the new day will be worthwhile just to get up out of bed each morning," Elton volunteered. "We have to have faith we can prepare and give interesting, relevant, and solid lectures. Heck, to stay in school as long as we did and endure so many classes taught by losers and jerks required great faith we could one day become fine teachers and make a meaningful difference in *our* students' lives."

"It sure took a lot of faith to get me through graduate school," Essielya offered. "With exceptions, I had so many professors who couldn't care less about teaching. They were obsessed with the next article or book they were working on and had so little time for students. Oh, they'd assign loads to read—much of it was theoretical garbage and political agitprop—but so many professors seemed to see teaching as a burden. Gosh, and the arrogance of some of them. To put it politely, they were pretty deficient in basic people skills."

"The two most important lessons I learned in graduate school"—Elton sighed—"were: one, how *not* to teach, and two, how *never* to treat people."

"Amen. I'm with you, Elton. Whenever I teach about a novelist or poet whose work some grad school professor did all he could to drain all the beauty, artistry, and mystery out of through endless political and 'cultural contextualization,' I resolve to do the opposite. And I have faith that I can too." She laughed.

The conversation eventually veered into their dating histories. Elton learned she had had a few long-term relationships but had not dated lately or ever married. Essielya learned of his few relationships and chortled at some of his embarrassing first date stories. Though part of him wondered if he was reverting to his performance mode, he decided not really since he was too relaxed and nothing felt forced.

To his delight, she shared some of her humorous dating adventures as well, which were even funnier. Both howled about the time a boyfriend grudgingly took her to the ballet but carried along a portable television set with a decent-sized screen so he could still watch his coveted ballgame during the performance—with the sound on and no headphones. Patrons seated near them promptly complained, and Essielya was thoroughly embarrassed. That was their last date.

But the funniest anecdote was the first date when the guy got arrested for driving under the influence of alcohol on the way to the restaurant, causing her to have to call a cab. That was also their last date.

"I was so angry and humiliated," Essielya managed to say between laughs.

Catching his breath, Elton asked, "Was he convicted?"

"I never cared to find out," she replied.

"But perhaps you could have been a character witness for him," Elton teasingly suggested.

"I would have testified for the prosecution. He knew better than to ask me for any help. Shoot, I should have sent that jerk the bill for the cab."

The conversation turned into a marathon talkfest, eventually extending a few hours, alternately philosophical, hilarious, and personal. Finally, after 1:00 a.m., they decided they better get some sleep since each had classes early in the morning and did not want to be too sleepy on their date. But it took Elton a long time to fall asleep. He was too excited and did not want to lose that dreamy sense of well-being which had returned. How he longed to drown in it.

Despite the lack of sleep, Friday's classes were fine. He did not have any new course preparations this term, so he enjoyed the confidence of delivering lectures whose fields he had plowed before. Plus, his fear of not doing well or appearing less than confident while delivering lectures was such that he always taught at a high energy level. Furthermore, he was too enthused about the date to be dragging. Though he had some of his usual first-date butterflies colliding in his stomach, he felt far fewer than before. Last night's record talkathon dispelled any remaining doubts about the sincerity of Essielya's interest in him. Though inevitably a little nervous about the possibility of disappointing her, he felt strongly they would at least remain dear friends which relaxed him considerably.

21
CHAPTER

Elton arrived at Essielya's apartment at six and was immediately struck by how splendid his date looked. She wore a lovely pink shirt with a red and gold flower design above a beautiful black skirt and shoes that resembled colorful Indian moccasins. She welcomed him inside to show the paintings and posters with which she had adorned her walls. After spending a half-hour discussing each, along with the contents of her very impressive book collection, they decided they better leave or they could easily miss dinner.

Though tempted to introduce her to perhaps the town's most popular restaurant, Mr. Allen's Grill, where she could meet the charming, witty, and legendary Mr. Allen himself, he chose the Thai place instead. Plenty of folks might recognize him at the Grill and he preferred keeping any dating relationship deep in the background. He especially did not want to risk students seeing them and starting rumors, particularly about the new English teacher eager to establish a solid reputation as a super instructor. Thai One On offered far more privacy and quiet.

The meal was excellent and they relaxed in a secluded booth in the back. Elton grew confident there might never be a struggle making interesting conversation with this wondrous lass. He relished not being so nervous or feeling pressure to impress. It was a relief to finally have a date who talked more than he did and was always intriguing too. Best of all, he rejoiced being comfortable enough to be fully frank about most anything.

Essielya was likewise grateful to finally be out with a man who was well groomed, dressed up for her, displayed courtly Southern manners, actually listened, maintained eye contact, and was consistently kind, interesting, and witty. She was further gratified he did not interrupt her, try to dominate the conversation, stare at other parts of her body, or make a pass. She felt emancipated to share almost anything with him as well. Indeed, his self-deprecating humor, ready acknowledgment of his own personal disappointments, and the sincere vibe she intuited from him convinced her he was completely trustworthy.

So when the talk turned to more personal struggles, she did not hesitate to confide how she had once had a drug problem for which she went to a rehabilitation center. Elton had met so many of her other hopes so far, she was optimistic he would be supportive regarding this revelation too. If not, why not find out now and not get any more emotionally attached?

As she shared how she got drawn into the addiction, Elton's eyes never left hers, he nodded when she wanted, and gently expressed how impressed he was she had courageously acknowledged and battled the problem and ultimately triumphed over it. She saw none of the sudden blinking of eyes, furtive glances elsewhere, or other signs of discomfort or disapproval she had encountered with some others when sharing her greatest struggle. Instead, Elton urged her to please seek him out if ever she wanted to talk about it or if he could help in any way.

"Thank you, Elton. I really appreciate that," she told him. "You're so sweet."

He was powerfully touched she chose to reveal such a private chapter of her life, and on a first date. It was hard to fathom they had only known each other for a few days since all their many hours of easy and intense conversations made him feel like he already understood her so well. And since she had taken such a risk to open up with her most deeply private struggle, he dared to do what he had never done with anyone outside his immediate family, pastor, and Beryl.

"You've been mighty frank and forthcoming with me, Miss Essielya, and I'm right honored and touched too. So since you've shared your most personal struggle with me, I'll share with you what I've never shared outside my tightest circle and never even with a girlfriend.

"Twelve years back, during my graduate school days—the worst of my life—I had what I was told was something of a nervous break-down while working on my master's thesis and ended up spending about a month in a psychiatric hospital out of state. It was real fright-ening, but I couldn't keep going the way I had since I think the name of the dead end street I was on was 'Suicide.' But I got some help and slowly climbed my way back to some kind of livable normal for me. The thesis got finished and I took the teaching gig which, though really scary at first for this shy boy, built up my confidence and pro-vided a sense of purpose by helping educate folks. My work's been a godsend. Still at night in bed I often think how far I've come, and it's as if I'm in a movie, and a really implausible one too. I've had tough times since and will always be shy and prone to anxiety, but I'm a heck of a lot better off than before."

"Bravo. I'm proud of you, Elton," Essielya declared. "How scared you must have been to go out of state by yourself to a hospital. And then to return to a small town not knowing if people had found out and how they'd react if they had. But you did what you needed to do and got a lot better for it."

"Thanks. Thanks very much."

"You know where to find me if ever you need a friendly ear," she said gently. Then, leaning across the table, "And our secrets are secure since we can now blackmail each other." She winked.

They both laughed and felt lighter. For the first time, there was a pause in their conversation, but it was not an uncomfortable one. Instead, they each smiled and enjoyed the other's gaze. Soon the chat picked up on much lighter topics where it remained for a while.

After all the straightforward revelations about past struggles and a suitable timeout for happier fare, Essielya decided perhaps this was an opportune time to inquire about the story she heard from a colleague concerning Elton's strange encounter in March. So after a rare pause during which she looked at him with a gentle smile, she asked, "How comfortable are you talking about your possible UFO experience?"

Elton blinked, sat up, and leaned back. Before this evening he had noted how grateful he was the subject had been absent from their extensive talks. He did not know if she was unaware of the incident, had purposely avoided bringing it up, or did not care. Based on her tremendous range of interests, he doubted the last option. He also recalled his last date falling apart when Kimberly asked about the encounter and he became convinced that was the real reason she went out with him. But Essielya had engaged him in many hours of wide-ranging conversations before broaching the topic and did so with light years' more respect and tact than Kimberly. And after they had been so open discussing the worst dramas of their lives, and had received only warm support from each other, replaying his spring encounter no longer felt out of bounds. Still, he was not expecting the question.

"Ah, that's...a big topic with many dimensions—no science fiction pun intended," he stammered and smiled nervously, glancing down at the table. Was he worried she might find his conduct that night cowardly? Why the sudden discomfort answering a question he no longer dreaded from students?

"Elton, I'm sorry. The last thing I want is to make you uncomfortable. Someone at the school mentioned it and so I was curious. I've long been fascinated by UFOs. But it's none of my business."

"You've done nothing wrong and have no need to apologize, Essielya. I'm doing a whole heck of a lot better about that drama than in the spring and early summer. It's just still something which causes some general anxiety. But as sweet and swell a listener as you've been and as relaxed as I am talking with you about everything else, I can't think of anyone off-hand with whom I'd rather share the tale. I'm so honored you shared your rehab experience, and you had the exact reaction to my mental hospital story that I hoped for. My little alien drama turned out to be not nearly as trying as that. Plus, there's a part of me that's glad you want to know about it. I've been getting better and better about the whole mess. And it has been over five months now. So I need to completely man up about it."

Reaching across the table to gently put her hand on his, she stated softly, "Please only share what you want and stop if it becomes the least bit of a drag. Trust me. I don't think we'll have trouble finding plenty of other topics to discuss." She grinned.

At the touch of her hand, he felt his entire being at peace. He smiled at her and told the whole tale, both the events of that long-ago Friday night and its painful, troubling aftermath. She listened without a single interruption before expressing how impressed she was with how well he handled the ordeal and honored she was he would share such a difficult personal story. She classified her own interest in UFOs as a subset of the general category of intriguing mysteries and eagerly joined him in speculating about what may have really happened that night. He was grateful retelling the story in such detail had not stirred up painful emotions as before and thanked her for being so kind.

They had been at the restaurant over two hours, but it was only 8:45. So Elton asked if she would like to inspect his collection of books and artifacts at home and meet the general. "Of course," she smiled, and they left the restaurant.

She was delighted with his books and pleased to see so many novels and collections of short stories and poems by many of her favorite authors. She also adored General Longstreet who was thrilled to meet someone new. He did not see many people and rarely ladies. When Elton tried to prevent him from jumping on her skirt, Essielya assured him that, having grown up on a farm with dogs of her own, she was happy he was elated to see her. So they went in the backyard to play fetch with the general. Though it was nighttime, there was a full moon and his dog had no trouble finding the tennis ball with every throw.

Looking toward the woods, Essielya grew pensive, then smiled and looked at Elton for a while. He smiled back inquisitively.

"So that's where the most eventful night of your life occurred," she stated while arching an eyebrow.

"Yes. Right out there not too far from those trees," he replied.

"I think it's so cool you had the guts to return to the clearing with Beryl and your dog."

"I wouldn't have gone without them or at night."

Then she tilted her head a tad to the side, and her smile grew into a full grin. Her brilliant blue eyes were bathed by the moonlight and now appeared as sapphires. It dawned on him what she was proposing. While he felt some apprehension, he saw the chance for a special adventure which might not only be fun, but an opportunity to further defeat his fears. And life had taught him the worst regrets were missed opportunities, and this moment struck him as mighty enticing.

"Are you daring me?"

"Only if you want, Elton. Please, no pressure. I enjoy being with you anywhere."

He felt his heart melt again and looked at the dark trees to his left. Slowly a smile formed, and he turned back to Essielya.

Pretending to be scared, he asked, "Only if you hold my hand."

"Absolutely." She laughed. "You'll be my hero."

"It might make a pretty unique first date experience, huh?"

"It would jump to the top of mine." She chuckled.

"Let me get the flashlight and the general's leash. What do you know, boy, we're going back to the clearing."

Returning with the flashlight, Elton put Longstreet on the leash, which excited him tremendously. It was a new thrill for him to get to leave the yard at night.

"I am *so* stoked," Essielya whispered. "This is *incredibly* cool."

To his relief, Elton was not too nervous. Rather, he sensed this was a rare chance to create a really positive and memorable experience while conquering another hurdle. To reassure himself further, he got Essielya's agreement that, if they encountered anything or anyone in the woods, they would immediately return. Both shuddered and laughed at the thought of bumping into any students making a pilgrimage to "the UFO site."

So the three of them set off into the woods. She held the general's leash, and the dog happily took the lead. Elton held the flashlight straight ahead. It was dark, but the glow of the bright moon through a cloudless sky helped their vision as they slowly started forward. Without warning, Elton felt Essielya slip her hand in his. Before he could catch himself, he looked at her in surprise. She returned his look with a gaze of contentment. Though he could not deny he still had some fear, he now felt stronger and far from alone.

For the first time since they met, the silence between them lasted a full minute. But the grip of the other's hand and the excitement running through them more than compensated. They turned to each other and erupted laughing at each one's look of childlike wonder mixed with a dose of suspense. Elton remarked how good it felt to hear the crickets in contrast to the last time he explored these woods at night. Also, unlike before, the only lights came from the moon, the stars, and their flashlight.

General Longstreet wagged his tail briskly but did not bark, and he continued leading them in a straight line as he had with Elton and Beryl. The journey remained slow due to the thickness of trees, so much brush, and lack of a path. But each enjoyed the adventure.

When they suddenly heard leaves rustle to their right, they each stopped and turned. Elton immediately pointed the flashlight in that direction to reveal nothing unusual, prompting Essielya to lean into him laughing at how scared they had been.

"Your eyes looked so big just now, Elton."

"I was just concerned you might be frightened," he deadpanned with a slight smile.

"Uh-huh. Right."

As they continued, Elton reflected on how very far he had come over the last five months. He now felt almost no fear and was instead speculating on what new spray-painted messages and other visitors' souvenirs they might find. He also regretted forgetting to bring a garbage bag to recycle all those beer bottles.

"Mr. Peabody, I just want you to know how much I appreciate you showing me all around my new town."

"I just want to give you the full tour, dear."

Elton wanted to delay arriving at the clearing so the experience could last as long as possible. How bizarre and alternately terrifying, hilarious, and strangely ironic life can be, he pondered.

"What are you smiling about, Mr. Peabody?"

"Huh? I didn't even realize I was. I'm just tickled to be here with you, Miss McGahee. And I feel like we're young teenagers up to mischief."

"I know. Me too. What a hoot."

Soon they could see what appeared to be an opening in the trees ahead. Elton remarked how vastly different the sight was this evening compared with the last night he was here. And unlike when he and Beryl made the trek, General Longstreet did not start lunging ahead or barking. Instead he maintained his carefree pace, wagging his tail.

Elton described how brightly lit even the backsides of trees close to the clearing were that other night and how refreshingly dark they were now. She squeezed his hand and smiled at him.

When they reached the opening, it struck him how the place was still lit, but this time just by the moon's glow and his flashlight. There were the same beer cans and bottles, as well as the campfire sight. To his delight, the goofy spray-painted messages remained, albeit paler now. They looked all the funnier at night, and Essielya and Elton fell into a giggling fit over them that was partly an expression of relief that everything else about the spot was utterly typical. It appeared they were the first visitors since he, Beryl, and the general had made their sojourn there over two months before. The dog still loved racing around the clearing, stopping to sniff each can and bottle, and marking his territory here and there.

After inspecting the whole site still holding hands, Elton and Essielya stood at the center to peer in every direction before finally looking into each other's eyes. Both smiled, neither needing to talk. Then Essielya spoke.

"A penny for Mr. Elton's thoughts now that he has faced his biggest fear by returning to the scene of his most important encounter. And your palm only sweated way back before we even got here…and some of the sweat may have been mine." She giggled.

He took in the entire scene and thought, occasionally looking at her gazing at him. The general sat by him, and he rubbed his head.

"Life remains both a massive mystery and irony. Here's the scene of the most bizarre, chilling encounter I've ever had and which I still don't understand. But standing here now…with you…it just doesn't even seem to matter anymore. I sure don't ever want to have another like it. But if it led to tonight's experience here with you, then it was all worth it."

She gave him a hug, and they held each other. There was so much he wanted to say, but words were no longer needed. He just wanted to bask in this moment as long as possible.

Have I finally found the soul mate I've always dreamed about? Essielya wondered. She no longer felt any need to talk either but just wanted them to bathe together in this moonlight the whole night.

He looked in her eyes and remarked how stellar they appeared. She grinned and embraced him tighter. He stared up at the moon and appreciated its beauty and mystery as never before.

"Has the moon ever looked more fetching?" he asked.

Turning her gaze upward, she sighed. "Never."

Elton looked at Essielya's fabulous face staring above and thought she had never looked more enchanting. He slowly leaned in and kissed those lusciously large lips and luxuriated in the warm, wet welcome she gave him. They explored each other's mouth much more thoroughly than they had the entire clearing, and both felt a sense of bliss they had never known. Nothing else seemed to matter anymore. Neither had ever expected to meet someone who fulfilled so many wants. When they finally broke for air, each gazed into the other's eyes while nuzzling their noses. At last Elton spoke.

"Miss Essielya, thank you for helping transform this place from the site of my worst encounter to the site of my best. And *this* is now my most important encounter of all."

Essielya McGahee grinned wider than ever as they resumed their kiss. She could not recall when she had felt more at peace. And this was a whole new reality for Elton Peabody.

The End

ABOUT THE AUTHOR

Photo by Alexandra
Zak-Johnson

Born in Bartow, Florida, in 1961, Dr. Douglas Young was reared a faculty brat in Athens, Georgia, before becoming a full-time professional nerd himself. He taught political science and history at Gordon College in Barnesville, Georgia, from 1987 to 1999. He then taught at Gainesville State College in Gainesville, Georgia, from 1999 to 2013, and he taught at the University of North Georgia-Gainesville from 2013 until his retirement at the end of 2020. He also advised UNG's Politically Incorrect and Chess Clubs. Many of his essays and poems have appeared in a variety of publications.